A Frosty Fright

Heading their way, its skin glowing an eerie white, was an enormous worm. As it slithered through the underground passage, the tunnel's foundations began to shift. With each contraction of its body, another beam support cracked.

"I don't believe it!" Kellach cried. "What would a frost worm be doing down here?"

"What can we do to fight a frost worm?" Moyra yelled over the growing rumble.

"Run!" Kellach shouted. "If that thing catches up to us, it will swallow us whole!"

BOOK 1
SECRET OF THE SPIRITKEEPER

BOOK 2
RIDDLE IN STONE

BOOK 3
SIGN OF THE SHAPESHIFTER

BOOK 4
EYE OF FORTUNE

BOOK 5
FIGURE IN THE FROST

FIGURE IN THE FROST

LANA PEREZ

KNIGHTS OF THE SILVER DRAGON

BOOK 5

COVER & INTERIOR ART
EMILY FIEGENSCHUH

MIRROR STONE

Figure in the Frost
©2005 Wizards of the Coast, Inc.

Distributed in the United States by Holtzbrinck Publishing. Distributed in Canada by Fenn Ltd.

Distributed to the hobby, toy, and comic trade in the United States and Canada by regional distributors.

Distributed worldwide by Wizards of the Coast, Inc. and regional distributors.

Cover and interior art by Emily Fiegenschuh
Cartography by Dennis Kauth
First Printing: February 2005
Library of Congress Catalog Card Number: 2004113689

9 8 7 6 5 4 3 2 1

US ISBN: 0-7869-3587-1
ISBN-13: 978-0-7869-3587-1
620-17644-001-EN

U.S., CANADA,
ASIA, PACIFIC, & LATIN AMERICA
Wizards of the Coast, Inc.
P.O. Box 707
Renton, WA 98057-0707
+1-800-324-6496

EUROPEAN HEADQUARTERS
Wizards of the Coast, Belgium
T Hofveld 6d
1702 Groot-Bijgaarden
Belgium
+322 457 3350

Visit our website at **www.mirrorstonebooks.com**

For those who fight to keep magic in our world

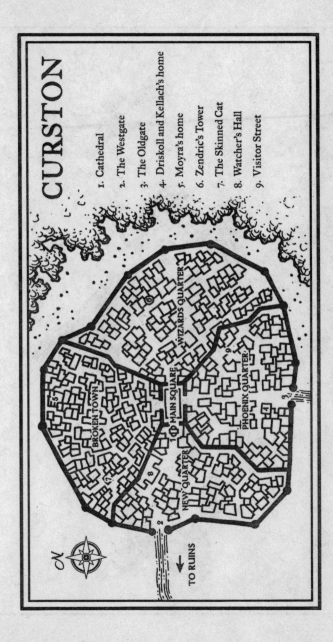

CURSTON

1. Cathedral
2. The Westgate
3. The Oldgate
4. Driskoll and Kellach's home
5. Moyra's home
6. Zendric's Tower
7. The Skinned Cat
8. Watcher's Hall
9. Visitor Street

CHAPTER

1

I'll build a snow wizard and a snow castle, and then Driskoll, Kellach, and I will have a huge snowball fight."

Moyra stood in front of her mother's stand in Curston's market, dancing from foot to foot. Snowflakes dotted her scarlet hair, and her nose was red with cold.

Early that morning, snow had blanketed the town of Curston for the first time in over a hundred years. Now, it seemed everyone in Curston was in the market, buying cold weather supplies.

Merchants had brought out velvet cloaks, woolen coats, and other warm winter clothes. The scent of steaming soups and hot chocolate wafted over the tents and stalls that lined the edge of Main Square. Hundreds of people filled the rows of stands, haggling over furry coats, hats, and hot food.

"So, do I have to help you today?" Moyra asked her mother for the fourth time. Normally she didn't mind helping her mother sell her crafts at the stand in the market, but today was different. Today was a snow day!

"When it snows there's just so much to do!" Moyra said. "And there's no telling how long the snow will be here. You don't want me to miss out on the only snow day in my entire lifetime, do you?"

"There'll be plenty of time for that nonsense soon enough," Royma snapped. "But now there's work to be done." Royma lifted a wooden crate onto one of the tables in the back of her stand. The box overflowed with knitted scarves in shades of bilious green, mustard yellow, and sienna brown. "I was up all night knitting these scarves."

Moyra wrinkled her nose. "Those are the ugliest scarves I've ever seen, Mom."

Royma shrugged. "The yarn was a good value. And besides, no one seems to care what color they are. They just want something warm to get them through this weather. I've already sold one crate full."

A chill wind blew through Moyra's thin jacket. She wrapped her arms tighter around her chest. "I miss Daddy. He would take me sledding."

"I know it's not much fun to work in this stand." Royma turned to face Moyra, her hands on her hips. "But I'm doing all I can to put food on the table. And that's more than I can say for your thieving father. That man would rather rot in jail than do an honest day's work."

"It wasn't Daddy's fault that he was arrested again." Actually Moyra knew it was her father's fault, but she would never admit it to anyone, even to her own mother. Moyra's father, Breddo, was born a thief and would probably die a thief. The trouble

2

was he just wasn't a very good thief.

Royma gave a deep sigh. "I don't want to hear another word about it. This is the busiest the market's been in months, and we've got work to do." Royma pointed to the shovel leaning against the edge of the stall. "Clear out the snow in front of the stand while I unload the rest of the scarves from this box."

"Fine." Moyra gripped the shovel's handle and dug into the pile of fluffy snow at her feet. Her hands were already stiff from the freezing cold, and the snow was heavy. Even though it had only been snowing for half the day, a huge pile had already settled against the rickety wooden stand. The drifts covered her feet, and the snowflakes were still coming down fast.

After several minutes, Moyra was relieved to hear her mother's voice calling from the back of the stall. "Look alive, girl! We've got a customer!"

Moyra turned. A tall boy dressed in wizard's apprentice robes was approaching the stand.

"Kellach!" Moyra called. "What are you doing here? I thought you had your lesson at Zendric's today." Kellach was apprenticed to Zendric, the oldest and wisest wizard in all of Curston.

"Zendric said there wasn't much point in studying on a day like today. So we walked over here and he bought me some hot chocolate! Want some?" Kellach lifted a steaming cup and Moyra inhaled the delicious scent.

Before she could answer, Zendric walked up and placed another steaming cup in Moyra's hand. "There's one for you, too." The old wizard's eyes crinkled as he smiled.

Moyra's fingers tingled against the hot cup. The steam warmed her face as she sipped.

Royma rushed to the front of the stand. "Hello, Zendric!" Her voice took on a sugary spin. "May I interest you in a fine woolen scarf?" Royma lifted a bright yellow and brown scarf up to Zendric's face.

Zendric lifted one eyebrow. "Uh, nothing for me today, Royma. But I see your stand is doing brisk business."

Royma scowled. "For today at least. But I'm almost out of yarn, and it doesn't look like this snow will be stopping any time soon. If the supply wagons don't arrive tomorrow, I could be out of business. I hear there are even winter wolves circling outside Curston's walls. One of my customers said he heard them howling last night."

Zendric took in a quick breath. "Winter wolves? In Curston?"

"Yes, indeed," Royma said. "I've never heard of such creatures in our region. Normally, the winter wolves live far to the north. It's probably just a rumor, but it's strange, isn't it?"

"Yes, it is strange," Zendric said, rubbing his chin. "Strange indeed." He fell silent, staring off into the distance.

Driskoll, Kellach's younger brother, came running up. "Kellach! Moyra! I've been looking all over for you. They've closed off the plaza in front of the cathedral, and it's the perfect spot to build snow forts. Meet you there."

And without another word, Driskoll went racing off toward the cathedral at the west end of Main Square

Kellach looked up at Zendric. "If it's all right with you?"

4

The question seemed to snap Zendric out of his daydream. "Yes, yes, certainly. You're dismissed for the day. I've got some business to attend to." Zendric began to step away from the stand.

Then quite suddenly, he stopped and turned around, pulling a small red book from inside his robes. "In the meantime, I expect you to study this."

"Aw, more homework?" Kellach said. "It's a snow day!"

"Guard it well." Zendric leaned over and put the book in Kellach's hand. "I'm counting on you, boy."

Kellach rolled his eyes and, nodding, tucked the book into one of the pouches on his belt.

Moyra set her now empty cup on the counter. "Mom, can I go too?"

Royma's mouth opened, already forming a no, but then her eyes caught Zendric's. "I suppose. But be home by dark, if you know what's good for you."

"Thanks, Mom!" Moyra shouted, and she and Kellach raced to the cathedral, catching snowflakes with their tongues.

When they arrived, they found Driskoll patting a pile of snow into a lopsided wall in front of the cathedral steps. A silly grin covered his face when he caught sight of his brother and Moyra. "It's about time! I'm almost finished with Fort Driskoll."

"Driskoll, that's not how you build a snow fort," Kellach said loftily as he stomped closer to Driskoll's creation. "I have a better idea. Let me show you—"

But before Kellach could finish, Driskoll reached over and threw a handful of snow down the front of Kellach's robes.

5

"Hey!" Kellach shouted, jumping forward and shaking out his robes. "What'd you have to do that for?"

"It was a surprise attack." Driskoll giggled. "At least there's *one* thing I can do better than you!"

"Snowball fight!" Moyra cried. She threw a softly packed snowball at Driskoll. Driskoll dodged, but not fast enough. The snow smacked against his jacket.

"I'll get you for that!" Driskoll scooped up a handful of snow and sprinkled it in Moyra's hair.

Kellach grinned. "Okay, you two want a snowball fight? I'll give you a snowball fight. Watch this!" Kellach closed his eyes and recited something under his breath. His hand waved, and a ray of frost flew through the air. It was the brightest snow Moyra had ever seen, so white it looked like sugar flying through the sky.

Kellach stepped back a little, into the shadow of the cathedral. The ray of frost zoomed toward a huge bank of snow, next to Driskoll's fort.

The icy ray hit the bank, and the pile of snow exploded.

"Aaaahhh!" Driskoll cried, diving behind his half-ruined fort. "Okay, I give up! I give up!"

Kellach turned to Moyra, smiling. "Now it's your turn."

Moyra laughed. "I'm not afraid of your frost ray spell, Kellach!" She ran closer to the cathedral. "You can't catch me."

"Okay, no frost rays. How about this instead?"

Kellach muttered under his breath again. The snowflakes at Kellach's feet swirled in a circular motion and then bunched together to form a snowball, the biggest snowball Moyra had ever seen. It was as big as a barrel and it looked just as heavy. As Kellach lifted his hand, it began to roll.

"Kellach, no!" Moyra laughed and ducked behind one of the cathedral's columns.

The snowball thumped against the tower column, shaking the stone as it hit.

"Hah! You missed!" Moyra called. She looked down at her feet. Lying on the ground were two snowballs. One was the giant magic snowball Kellach had made. The other was small, only about the size of her fist. Moyra was sure Kellach had thrown only one snowball at her. Where had the other one come from?

Just then, a voice called from the edge of the cathedral grounds. "Driskoll! Kellach!" Moyra looked up to see Torin, Kellach and Driskoll's father, calling across the snow-covered plaza.

Tall and burly, Torin marched resolutely across the plaza. His tall captain's boots crunched in the snow as he walked.

"Royma told me I'd find you boys here," Torin said when he reached them.

Driskoll's head popped up from behind his fort. "Aw, Dad. Do we have to go? We were just having the *best* snowball fight."

Torin nodded and pointed to the sky. "I'm afraid so. It's almost curfew, and this storm is getting worse."

Moyra looked at the darkening sky and was surprised to see it was almost nightfall. Her mother would be closing up the stall by now. Moyra felt guilt course through her body. There was barely any food in the cupboard, and she had run off to play with Driskoll and Kellach. If she hurried, she would get back to the market at least in time to help her mother clean up.

"You coming, Moyra?" Driskoll asked as Kellach and Torin stomped off ahead of him.

Moyra nodded absently. But then she caught sight of the strange snowball at her feet. "Uh, go ahead without me. I just want to, um, clear some of this snow off the cathedral steps."

"Suit yourself!" Driskoll said and ran off to catch up with his brother.

As soon as Driskoll was out of sight, Moyra leaned over to pick up the small ball of snow. It felt too heavy for a regular snowball. She rubbed the snow off and saw what looked like hard dirt. This wasn't just a regular snowball, she quickly realized. There was something inside the snowball. A lump of mud? A rock maybe?

She tapped the hard ball against the column, and bit by bit the dirt flaked away. On one side, Moyra thought she could see something shiny underneath.

Moyra felt butterflies rising in her stomach. Maybe she would find something in this snowball she could sell at the market. What if someone had dropped a golden coin and it had somehow gotten swept up in the snowstorm? If she found a coin, there was no harm in keeping it, was there? A smile crossed Moyra's face as she nodded to herself. Finders keepers, as her father always said.

With one final thwap against the stone column, the last bit of dirt fell away.

Moyra gasped.

What she held in her hand wasn't a snowball. It wasn't a rock. Or even a golden coin.

It was a diamond. A diamond as big as a goose egg.

Moyra sat down on the cathedral steps and stared at the gem in her hand, not even feeling the snow seep through her clothes.

The stone gleamed with blue light. Her heart beat hard, and her mind raced.

A diamond like this would feed her family for years. She would never have to work in the market again. When her father got out of prison, he wouldn't have to steal for a living. She would buy her mother a new dress. She would have new clothes. Maybe they'd be able to move out of Broken Town and into the New Quarter or even the Phoenix Quarter, where Kellach and Driskoll lived.

Moyra's first impulse was to visit one of her father's friends in Broken Town. One of Breddo's friends was sure to know where to sell a jewel like this, no questions asked. She jumped to her feet, and began to run, then suddenly she stopped.

Someone might not miss a lost coin, but a gem like this would certainly be missed. What if someone were searching for it right now? If anyone saw her with this jewel, would she be accused of stealing it? She looked down and took in the blue glow of the giant gem. Or what if it were cursed? Moyra shuddered at the thought.

Moyra placed the diamond in the drawstring pouch where she kept her coins and tucked the leather pouch into her jacket.

She'd keep the diamond a secret, just a little while, until she could find out more about it.

She'd lived her whole life in Broken Town. Why not a few days more?

CHAPTER

2

The next morning, Moyra yawned as she hurried across Main Square.

Her mother had dragged her to the market at the crack of dawn and forced her to shovel snow out of the stall. Moyra had almost told her mother about the gem right then. But she immediately thought better of it. Royma would think that the diamond had been stolen. She'd probably call the watchers herself, Moyra thought bitterly.

Moyra was glad, at least, that her mother hadn't made her stay at the stand all day. Her two pairs of socks and her boots weren't nearly enough to keep out the cold. She wrapped her new scarf tighter around her neck. When her mother had seen her shivering in the snow, she'd insisted she take it. It was bile green, the worst color of the lot, and it itched her neck. But Moyra had to admit it was warm. And it wouldn't be long before she could buy herself a beautiful purple one, made of the finest wool in the land.

The wind picked up, blowing hard snow in her face. The snow had fallen off and on all night and the snow drifts were now up to Moyra's knees. Moyra trudged a well-worn path through the drifts past the obelisk at the center of Main Square. The central plaza was much less crowded today. Probably most people were staying inside, trying to keep warm.

As she rounded the obelisk, she saw Driskoll and Kellach. She waved and they rushed over.

"Nice scarf," Driskoll said, pointing at the bilious green thing wrapped around Moyra's neck. "Did you lose your lunch on it?"

Moyra tightened her lips. "It's all I have, okay?" Her hand gestured toward Driskoll's and Kellach's expensive woolen coats. "Some of us don't have the money to buy everything we want. We have to take what we can get."

"Sorry." Driskoll held up his hands defensively. "It was just a joke." He began to wiggle out of his heavy coat. "If you want, you can wear my coat. I think it's ugly too."

Moyra waved away the offer. "No, no. It's all right." She brushed the snowflakes off her arms and sighed. "I'm sorry. This weather must be getting to me. I'm sick of being cold." She wrapped her arms around herself.

Kellach kicked a snowdrift. "Yeah, it's strange, isn't it? It doesn't seem natural."

"What does Zendric make of it?" Moyra asked.

"I don't know," Kellach said. "I haven't seen him. He sent me a message saying he was canceling my lessons for a few days."

Moyra cocked her head. "Why do you think he did that?"

She shifted a little, and a hard edge of the diamond dug into her skin.

Kellach shook his head. "I thought it was because of the weather. I don't remember Curston ever being this cold."

Driskoll said, "I hope he's not sick."

Kellach looked at his brother in alarm. "I hope not either."

"Maybe he's sick, like everyone else in Curston. Sick of the cold that is," Moyra said.

"We should go visit him," Driskoll said impulsively. "Dad gave me some extra money. I'll use it to buy Zendric some hot soup. Want to come with us?"

Moyra shrugged. "I don't know. I was on my way home."

"Come on." Driskoll tugged on her jacket. "We'll buy you a hot chocolate on the way, right, Kell?"

Moyra sighed. Once she sold her diamond, she could afford hot chocolate any time she wanted. But for now, it was hard to turn down the offer. "All right," she said.

As they headed back to the market, Moyra noticed that the people of Curston were finding creative ways to stay warm. One woman was bundled in so many scarves that you could only see her eyes. Moyra laughed out loud when she saw a dwarf waddle by wearing several layers of pants.

Kellach ordered three hot chocolates with double chocolate and double cream at the sweets stand.

The elf maiden nodded and headed for the cauldron at the back.

But she returned with only two steaming mugs. "Sorry, children. We've only enough chocolate for two."

"You've got to be kidding!" Moyra said. "How could you be out of chocolate?"

The elf shrugged. "The supply wagons didn't arrive this morning. People are saying they may not arrive at all today. Until then, no more chocolate."

"Here." Driskoll handed Moyra one of the two cups. "You can drink this one while I go get Zendric's soup."

Moyra started to protest but Driskoll was already running off. "It's only fair!" he called.

As Moyra and Kellach sipped their hot chocolate, they noticed a small crowd gathered around the booth next door. They set their empty mugs on the sweets stand and squeezed through the crowd to get a closer look.

The vendor, a large gnome with silver hair, was waving his arms, trying to calm the crowd. "One at a time, one at a time. Only twenty-five silvers a piece."

"I'll give you thirty!" a large half-orc woman yelled.

The stall was strewn with patchwork caps, made of slime green, shocking purple, and glaring red.

Kellach wrinkled his nose. "Those caps smell!"

"And they're hideous," Moyra said. "I can't believe anyone would pay one silver for those old rags."

The merchant leaned over and whispered, "Haven't you heard, children? The cold snap is expected to continue. Curston is running out of firewood, and the supply wagons are delayed. People will buy anything to keep warm. I made these out of my dirty bed linens. But do these people care?" The merchant rubbed his hands together gleefully. "Supply and demand, children. Supply and demand." He turned back to the crowd and shouted, "Warm caps! Get them while they last!"

"What's going on?" Driskoll came up behind them, carrying a lidded ceramic pot.

"You don't want to know." Kellach shook his head and changed the subject. "What kind of soup did you get?"

Driskoll opened the lid a crack. "It's beef and potato stew. The vendor said to keep the lid on and it would stay warm. But I have to return the pot tomorrow." A rich beefy scent wafted out of the small pot.

Moyra's stomach grumbled. She couldn't remember the last time she'd tasted meat on her lips. When she sold the diamond, she and her mother would be able to eat beef every night.

"You've got to smell this, Kellach." Driskoll held out the pot to his brother. As he did, he slid on a patch of ice.

"Mind the soup!" Moyra said and grabbed him by the arm to steady him.

"I didn't spill a drop," Driskoll said, finally regaining his footing and replacing the lid.

Moyra looked at the liquid dribbling down the side of the pot. "Right. Not a drop."

"Let's get that soup to Zendric before you spill the whole thing," Kellach said.

Moyra's stomach twisted at the mention of Zendric's name. She no longer felt hungry. What if he knew something about the diamond? What if he knew where it came from? What if he said the diamond was cursed and it would hurt someone?

But at the same time she kept thinking, the diamond won't hurt anyone. It will help someone. It will help *me*.

She put her hand in her pocket and felt the jewel, wrapped snugly in her leather pouch She took a deep breath and came to a decision. There was only one way to settle this. She had to show Zendric the diamond and ask him what he knew about it. If he didn't know anything, it was hers for the keeping. That was fair. It was what a real Knight of the Silver Dragon would do. Instantly, her stomach settled and she felt better.

A few moments later, they reached Zendric's tower. They slipped through the gate and Kellach rapped on the huge door.

But there was no answer. Kellach hesitated, uncertain what to do next.

"Where could he be?" Moyra asked.

"Maybe he's too sick to come to the door," Kellach said.

"Do you have a key?" Driskoll asked.

"No, but it might be unlocked." He twisted the handle. The door opened easily.

There was no fire in the fieldstone fireplace, and the air in the room was freezing. The overstuffed chairs sat primly, as if waiting for callers. The worktable was piled high with vellum scrolls.

But there was no sign of Zendric.

CHAPTER

3

The three kids searched the tower thoroughly, but they didn't find a note from Zendric.

Driskoll set the pot of steaming soup down on Zendric's worktable. He sat down in one of the tall wooden chairs, pulled a wooden spoon from his pocket, and began slurping the stew.

Moyra built a small fire in the stone fireplace, then settled in an armchair in front of the hearth.

"Mmm, delicious." Driskoll lifted his wooden spoon out to his brother. "Kellach, want some?"

But Kellach didn't seem to hear him. "This isn't like Zendric at all," he said, pacing up and down the room. "Zendric takes his responsibilities very seriously. He would never deliberately worry any of the Knights of the Silver Dragon." There was a note of panic in his voice.

"I don't know," Moyra said, warming her hands in front of the crackling fire. "Zendric doesn't tell us everything. Maybe he decided to, uh, go on vacation? Get away from the cold?"

"But he would tell us if he went away," Kellach said.

"At least if he could tell us," Driskoll added.

A shiver ran down Moyra's back. "Do you think Zendric's in danger?"

Kellach turned and looked her directly in the eye. "I'm not sure," he said solemnly, "but I think we need to find out."

Kellach rubbed his chin, his eyes fixed on the floor. "We need to think this through logically."

"Start with the last time you heard from Zendric," Driskoll said, his mouth half full with soup. "What did he say?"

"He sent me a message canceling my lessons."

Driskoll paused, the spoon halfway to his mouth. "Right! What did it say? Maybe that was a clue!"

Kellach looked at Driskoll. "It said, 'I am canceling your lessons for the next few days.'"

Driskoll slumped his shoulders. "Oh."

Moyra crossed her arms in front of her chest. "The message wasn't really the last thing he *said* to you. The last time you talked was—"

"At the market!" Kellach shouted, suddenly remembering.

"What did he say?" Driskoll leaned forward in his chair.

"He said something about studying and . . ." Kellach's face reddened. "I completely forgot. He gave me this." He pulled the tiny red book out of a pouch on his belt. "And then he said, 'Guard it well.'"

"Hah!" Driskoll said, jumping up from his chair. "I knew it! It *is* a clue."

18

"Guard it well?" Moyra asked. "What's that supposed to mean?"

Kellach shrugged. "I thought he was just being dramatic. To get me to study." Kellach flipped the book over in his hands.

"Maybe he meant you were supposed to guard the book?" Moyra said. "As in don't lose it?"

Kellach wrinkled his forehead. "I've never lost anything of Zendric's. That doesn't make much sense."

"What's the title of the book? Maybe that will help." Driskoll leaned forward to get a better look. "Aw, it's in Elvish. Can you read it, Kell?"

"Of course!" Kellach scoffed. "It's simple." He pointed to the two squiggles embossed into the leather on the front of the book and put on his best teacher's voice. "You see, that's the symbol for fire. And this one . . . uh, this says something about gems."

"Gems? Like diamonds?" Moyra's chest felt tight. The diamond jabbed into her side.

"No, not gems," Kellach said. "It's a different word. Amulets. Fire amulets, yes, that's it." He looked up triumphantly.

Moyra felt the breath whoosh out of her. She had nothing to worry about. Zendric had nothing to do with the diamond.

She stared at the book cover. "I've seen something like those symbols before," she said.

"Where?" Driskoll asked.

She squinted her eyes. "If only I could remember . . ."

Driskoll turned to his older brother. "So Zendric gave you a book about fire amulets? What are fire amulets anyway?"

"They're magical protective weapons, crafted by elves." Kellach opened the cover of the book. "Now give me a few minutes, and I'll prepare a full summary of the contents of this book. It shouldn't take me long to translate it." Kellach put his finger on the first page and began reading to himself.

Moyra slumped back in Zendric's chair and hugged her knees to her chest, trying to remember where she'd seen those symbols before. Was it somewhere in Broken Town? No. At Watchers' Hall? No. She listed all the places she could think of, but it was no use. She couldn't remember.

The clock ticked in the quiet room, marking off every moment. Kellach muttered under his breath as he read. Finally, Moyra couldn't stand the wait any longer.

She sat up. "Well, what does it say?"

Kellach looked up sheepishly. "I've got the first sentence: 'Fire amulets are danger . . . dangerous weapons.' See?" He pointed to a squiggle on the first line of the book. "That's the symbol for danger."

"And then what?"

Kellach bent over the book, not wanting to meet her eyes. "I've only got the first sentence."

"What happened to the full summary?"

"It was a bit more challenging than I expected, okay? But not to worry. I'll have this done in no time."

Moyra sighed, listening to the clock tick, until Kellach looked up again. "Okay, I've got the next sentence. 'There are . . . three amulets covered up . . . wait, no, hidden . . . in the . . . the city.'" Kellach grinned. "There are three amulets hidden in the city."

"What city?" Moyra asked.

"Here in Curston?" Driskoll asked.

Kellach shrugged. "I don't know. That might be in the third sentence." Kellach bent over the book and began reading again.

Moyra sighed. "It's going to take you all day just to translate the first page!"

"If you're so smart, why don't you translate it!" He tossed the book at her, and it landed in her lap.

"Come on, Kellach. That's not fair. I just meant maybe there might be a better way." Moyra picked up the book and rubbed her finger over the symbols on the cover.

"I know I've seen these somewhere before," she whispered to herself.

"Maybe we should go get Locky." Driskoll said.

Locky was Kellach's familiar, a clockwork dragon. As Kellach's familiar, he shared a magical bond with the apprentice wizard. Kellach could understand Locky's chattering language, read his thoughts, and sometimes even see through his eyes.

Kellach shook his head. "Locky only understands the language of the medusa, remember? He doesn't know Elvish. Besides, I don't want him out in this weather. The snow would ruin his gears."

"That's it!" Suddenly Moyra jumped to her feet. "The ruins!"

The two boys looked at her. "What about them?"

"I think that's where I saw that fire amulet symbol. We need to go to the ruins."

Driskoll groaned. "Not again. Remember the last time we were at the ruins? We almost got killed."

Kellach began pacing the room again. "And it's a three-mile walk," he added without looking up. "And it's still snowing."

Moyra remembered that it hadn't stopped snowing since she found the diamond. A quick tinge of guilt stabbed at her chest. Maybe it was cursed after all.

She stood in front of Kellach and waved the book in front of his face. "Now, listen to me. What if Zendric gave you this book because he wanted us to find those hidden amulets? If he is in danger, and if we find the amulets, maybe we'll be able to help."

Kellach nodded slowly.

She took a deep breath and continued, "The book said the amulets were hidden in the city. It's an old book, right? So it makes perfect sense that they were hidden in the old city! If Zendric's in danger, there's no time to waste. Come on, boys, we're Knights of the Silver Dragon. Real knights wouldn't let a little snow stop them."

Moyra tossed the tiny book back to Kellach. "Let's put it to a Silver Dragon vote. All in favor?"

CHAPTER

4

Outside the walls of Curston, the snow piled up in drifts as high as Moyra's head.

Their Silver Dragon vote had been unanimous, as Moyra knew it would be. Driskoll and Kellach would never turn down an opportunity for an adventure, no matter how cold it was outside.

They had decided to split up to get supplies and meet again by the Westgate in an hour. Moyra had hurried home and grabbed a knapsack filled with all sorts of supplies, as well as her father's coat and mittens. It was best to be prepared for anything when visiting the ruins.

As the three Knights headed down the road to the ruins, Moyra hunched against a chill wind. Even in her father's heavy coat, she felt as though the wind were blowing right through her. At least it had stopped snowing, she thought.

She concentrated on walking without slipping, placing one foot in front of the other, on the wide road. As she trudged along, she noticed that the beautiful white snow along the side of the road had turned a dirty gray.

Moyra took in a sharp breath. "The roads are clear."

"So?" Driskoll said.

"So why didn't the supply wagons reach Curston?" Moyra said.

Kellach stopped. "Listen!" he said.

They heard a faint howling sound coming from somewhere near the forest.

"Winter wolves," Driskoll said, drawing his coat tighter around him. "If we don't freeze to death out here, they're sure to eat us alive."

"Don't be silly. It's just the wind," Moyra said, but she shivered as she said it. "As long as we keep moving, we should be fine."

It took them much longer than usual to reach the ancient city, but they made their way up the final hill at last. Under a blanket of snow, the ruins looked almost peaceful. Still Moyra couldn't repress a shudder as she remembered all the frightening creatures they'd encountered here.

As she passed through the remains of the once legendary bronze gates, Moyra stopped suddenly.

"What's that?" she asked, pointing in the distance.

"What's what?" Kellach ran up beside her.

"Those towers. I've never seen those towers before." To the south, not far from the wide thoroughfare leading to Curston, three white turrets poked up through the trees.

Kellach rubbed his chin. "How strange." .

Driskoll huffed up beside them. "It looks like someone built a palace in the middle of the forest. But why would anyone want to live there? It's not exactly a friendly place."

Moyra wrapped her scarf tighter around her neck. "I don't know. Maybe it has something to do with Zendric."

Kellach nodded. "Let's look for the fire amulet symbol, then if we have time, we can investigate the towers on the way home."

Driskoll looked up at Moyra. "Where to?"

"It's just down the hill here. Not much farther." As she spoke, her breath formed frosty clouds in the air.

The Knights' feet made thick crunching noises as they walked down the hill and into the ruined city. Snowdrifts covered several of the buildings, disguising their disrepair.

"Walk carefully here," Moyra said. "The snow makes it hard to see."

"It looks so peaceful," Driskoll said.

"Well, it's not," Moyra warned.

After winding through the old streets for several minutes, Moyra came to a sudden stop before what once was an imposing building.

The roof of the building was long gone—now nothing more than a gaping hole. Wide stone steps led up to a platform filled with crumbled columns. There a marble lion stood watch beside the doorway. The door itself had long ago been reduced to a pile of timber, but the stone lion gleamed, as if it were brand-new.

Moyra took the steps two at a time. "This is it!" She shouted to the boys. "Come on! Hurry up."

"Look at the lion!" she said once Driskoll and Kellach had caught up to her. She took off her mittens and knelt by the statue. Emblazoned into the lion's chest was a large circular medallion. The edge of the circle was laced with small Elvish script, and in the center were two symbols just like the ones they'd seen on the cover of Kellach's book. "See! It says fire amulet, right, Kellach? I knew I'd seen those symbols before!"

"So now what?" Driskoll asked.

"Maybe this is the fire amulet?" She carefully wedged her fingers along the edges of the medallion and tugged. The stone cracked as the circular emblem began to give way.

Kellach shook his head. "The fire amulets are made of black stone. Not marble."

Moyra pushed her fingers farther into the crack she'd formed. "Well, maybe it's underneath here, then." Moyra looked over her shoulder at the boys. "It's coming loose."

Moyra tugged and tugged until at last the stone popped free, revealing a small cavity in the marble lion's chest.

Moyra peered inside the dark hole. "There's something inside." She poked her fingers into the compartment. Unlike the exterior of the lion, the stone here was rough. Her fingernails scrabbled against the edges of the cavity until at last she grasped something hard and cold.

She pulled it out. It was a smooth black rock, similar to a worry stone.

Kellach pointed to the symbol carved into the surface. "That's the Elvish symbol for fire."

"It's the amulet. I know it!" Moyra rubbed her forefinger

over a small hole at the top of the rock. "This must be where you string it through a chain."

"Here." He untied a long leather string from around his neck. "We can use this." He offered the leather thong to Moyra.

Moyra threaded the leather through the hole. She tied the ends together, knotting the leather firmly to create a makeshift necklace, and then held it out for Kellach.

He grasped hold of the necklace, but instead of putting it around his own neck, he motioned for Moyra to turn around.

She looked at him, puzzled. "Don't you want to keep it? It's magical, after all."

Kellach smiled. "Finders keepers."

Moyra's stomach twisted, and she remembered the diamond in her pocket. Moyra pasted a smile on her face that did not meet her eyes. "Yeah, finders keepers."

"Now turn around," he said. "Let me help you put it on." He pushed back her hair and lifted the amulet over her head.

"Hey, there's something else in here!" Driskoll called. His arm was stuffed inside the lion's chest. When he withdrew his fist, he had a tightly rolled scrap of parchment in his palm. He unrolled it. "It's written in Elvish, too." He looked at Kellach. "What do you think it says?"

Kellach took the parchment and looked at it closely, shaking his head. "Maybe it's a clue to find the next fire amulet? The book did say there were three."

Driskoll hopped to his feet. "Let's start searching!"

Kellach put a hand on Driskoll's shoulder. "Hang on, little

brother. There's not much point in searching until I can translate this clue."

"That might take a while." Moyra glanced at Driskoll and he smiled.

"Besides"—Moyra pointed up to the sky—"it's going to be dark soon, and if we're not back by curfew, your dad will be furious. Let's go check out those towers and then head home."

CHAPTER

5

They trudged back through the old city, past the main gate, and down the steep road. Normally, when they reached the end of this road, they would make a left onto the main thoroughfare back to Curston. But this time, led by Moyra, they took a sharp right.

They marched down the road for no more than a hundred paces, and then Moyra came to a sudden stop.

"Look! This is it." She pointed to a wide path through the trees. Her boots crunched in the snow as she barreled down the short path and into a large clearing, ringed by pines.

Moyra let out a gasp. The palace was even bigger than she had imagined. It glittered like crystal. The turrets went up and up, twisting and turning, until they seemed to pierce the cold winter sky.

Driskoll and Kellach came up behind her. "Where could it have come from?" Driskoll breathed.

"It must be magic," Moyra said. "Maybe this is where Zendric has been! A wizard had to have made this."

"It looks like it's made of glass," Kellach said.

"Or spun sugar," Moyra said dreamily.

"Let's go find out," Driskoll said.

"Be careful, Driskoll," Kellach warned.

Driskoll walked up to the front of the palace. Its double doors were as tall as giants and sat open as if in invitation to enter. At the center of each door was carved the image of a snarling wolf, with its nose acting like a door handle.

Driskoll slowly drew off his glove and put his hand to one wolf's smooth nose. His hand recoiled instinctively. "The door's made of ice," he called as he ran back to his brother and Moyra. "It looks like the whole place is."

"Wait until the people in town hear about this!" Moyra said. "People from all over the world will want to see a magical palace of ice."

"Magical?" Driskoll said. "Are you sure?"

"What else could it be?" Kellach answered the question. "Maybe Zendric did build it."

"Let's go inside and look for him." Driskoll said.

As they stepped over the threshold, Moyra couldn't help but gasp again. The palace was as amazing on the inside as it was on the outside.

The main room was an enormous space, as big as the Cathedral of St. Cuthbert. The ceiling soared high above their heads, and the room looked as if it could hold every person in Curston without being crowded.

Facing the entry was a fountain, all carved from ice, complete with jumping ice fish. A long banquet table, lined with delicate white chairs, sat in the center of the vast room.

Driskoll ran over to one of the chairs and sat down, only to jump up, startled. "Even the furniture is made of ice!" he said.

There was a vase of flowers on the table. The flowers were pink and looked so real. Moyra bent to smell their scent and screeched a little when their icy cold reached her nose.

"What kind of person could live in such cold?" Moyra wondered aloud.

Against the far wall, a large staircase curved upward.

"Hello!" Driskoll called out as they climbed the stairs. "Zendric? Hello? Is there anybody here?"

There was no answer.

At the top of the stairs, they pushed through a set of double doors and entered a narrow room. Glistening paintings of snarling wolves hung from the walls. Moyra stepped up to look at one painting and realized it wasn't a painting at all, but a flat slab filled with colored ice.

"Look at this!" Moyra turned and saw Kellach standing beside a wall lined with shelves. The shelves were filled with tiny glass globes of all sizes.

Kellach picked one up and shook it. "It's a snow globe!"

Moyra leaned closer. Inside the glass globe, tiny snowflakes floated around a miniature wagon. At the front of the wagon, stood two horses, carved in such detail that you could see the buckles on the bridles. The tiny wagon even had a driver: a green-skinned half-orc wearing a pointed hat.

"Amazing," she breathed. She looked back at the shelves. "They're *all* snow globes!" There were globes with miniature pixies, dwarves, elves, and even a few humans.

"They all look so real," Moyra said.

Driskoll shivered. "Come on, you two. There's no sign of Zendric, and it's freezing in here. Let's go home."

"You're right. Let's go." Reluctantly, Kellach set the glass globe back on the shelf and they headed down the stairs. They reached the entryway and walked out the doors with a sense of relief.

But when they emerged, the sky was a brooding black. The wind picked up and whipped through Moyra's hair. She felt cold air rushing through her heavy coat.

"Another storm is coming," Kellach said. "We'd better hurry."

They headed out through the path and onto the main thoroughfare back to Curston. But they'd only walked a few paces when Moyra spotted something.

"Is that a wheel?" She pointed at a clump of oak trees on the other side of the road. "Let's check it out," she said as she walked across the road.

"I'm freezing, Moyra," Driskoll whined. "Let's go!"

She ignored him and kept walking a few more yards until she reached the trees. There was something covered in a large canvas tarp.

She lifted the edge of the cloth and peered under. "What in the name of the gods!" she cried. She looked back at the boys. "It's one of the supply wagons."

Kellach and Driskoll came rushing up behind her.

"So this is why the supply wagons were delayed. She tugged at the tarp. "Help me pull this off. Maybe we can bring the supplies back to the city!" Together they pulled back the dirty canvas to reveal a battered wooden wagon.

But the wagon bed was completely empty. No yarn. No chocolate. No warm clothes or food. Nothing but a few specks of grain.

"How can this be?" Moyra said. "If the supplies never made it to Curston, where are they?"

Kellach rubbed his chin. "Someone must have stolen them."

Driskoll crouched down and ran his hand over the snow. "There aren't even any footprints in the snow." He stood up. "It's like the driver and the horses just disappeared into thin air."

"There's only one way someone can disappear into thin air," Kellach said, staring at his brother.

Driskoll's eyes widened. "Magic."

Kellach nodded. "This, my friends, is sabotage."

"You don't think Zendric had anything to do with this, do you?" Moyra asked.

"Impossible. If anything, Zendric was trying to stop whoever did this."

Kellach set the tarp back on top of the wagon and circled behind the back of the wagon. He squatted and peered closely at the wheel.

"There are usually two supply wagons," Moyra said. "One of them is still missing." She rushed back across the road. "We should search the woods." As she was about to plunge into a clump of trees, she heard what sounded like a low rumble.

"M-Moyra?" Driskoll called. "I think we should go."

"Quit whining, Driskoll. I know you're cold. But this is important."

"No, Moyra, I'm serious. W-w-we should go."

Moyra glanced over her shoulder at Kellach and Driskoll. They were both standing next to the wagon, right where she had left them. But their faces had blanched with fear, and they were staring at something down the road. Driskoll slowly lifted his arm and pointed.

The rumble sounded again, somewhere behind her. Then the rumble turned into a growl. She turned around.

Two winter wolves were pacing up the road toward them. One was about as tall as a pony, the other closer to the size of a large dog. Their white fur stood on end and their bared fangs dripped with drool. Their eyes gleamed red.

Moyra didn't move. She kept her eyes on the wolves, but out of the corner of her eye, she saw Driskoll start walking toward her.

"Driskoll, stay where you are," she called.

The larger animal sniffed the air. It gave one more growl and crouched low, baring its sharp, grisly teeth.

Then it leaped into the air, straight for Driskoll's throat.

CHAPTER

6

Moyra reached deep into her coat and grabbed the drawstring pouch where she kept the diamond. It was the heaviest thing she had handy. She swung the pouch by its strings. It made a satisfying clunk as it hit the pouncing wolf on the head.

The wolf yelped. It fell to the ground as Driskoll jumped back, just in time.

"Great shot, Moyra!" Driskoll said as he scurried closer. "I didn't know you had such a heavy purse! What's in there?"

"Just a . . . a rock I found." Moyra stuffed the purse back into her coat before Driskoll asked any more questions.

The large wolf whimpered and shook its head. But it wasn't long before its whimpers turned back into growls. It slowly rose to its feet again and began padding toward them. The small wolf circled behind them.

"They're surrounding us!" Moyra yelled. "Help, Kellach! Do something!"

"I'm working on it!" Kellach ran around the back of the

wagon onto the road. But he slipped on a patch of ice and fell on his back.

"Don't worry!" Driskoll stepped in front of Moyra and drew his sword. "I've got you covered." With a trembling hand, he slashed at the large wolf. The wolf leaned back and almost seemed to grin. It lifted one paw, and with a decisive swipe, it batted Driskoll's arm, sending his sword flying into the trees.

The big wolf snarled and padded closer.

"Quick!" Kellach called, scrambling to his feet. He had found a couple of stout branches that had fallen during the high winds. "Catch!" He tossed one to Moyra and then to Driskoll.

She caught the branch easily. She swung it in front of her with a warrior princess cry, "Aieeeeeya!"

But the wolves were not impressed. They only retreated a bit but didn't stop pacing a wide circle around them. Their large red tongues hung out of their mouths and drool dripped down.

"They look hungry," Driskoll said. "And they think we're dinner." He brandished his makeshift club.

As the small wolf snapped its jaws in a very unfriendly way, Moyra lifted her branch again and swung. "Aiyeee!"

The branch connected, hitting the growling animal on its snout. It yelped in pain and retreated.

The small wolf growled. And then it caught sight of Kellach.

"Kellach, watch out!" Driskoll called. The wolf leaped for Kellach's arm, but Kellach spun around just in time.

He swung his branch hard and connected with the wolf's chest. But this time, the blow only seemed to make the wolf angrier. Kellach backed up slowly. The wolf crouched low and gave a dangerous growl.

Suddenly Moyra remembered the amulet. She gripped the stone around her neck and, hoping it would work, shouted, "Fire!"

Nothing happened.

How does this thing work? Moyra thought. She wished she could read the Elvish words engraved on the amulet.

She held the necklace higher. "Fire! Fire!"

Still nothing happened.

"It's broken!" Moyra yelled. "The amulet's not working."

"Emalf!" Kellach shouted. "Emalf. Say Emalf!" The small wolf sprang at Kellach with its jaws snapping. He hit it with the branch again, but it hesitated only a moment before it moved in again to attack.

"Emalf," Moyra repeated quietly, pointing the amulet at the small wolf crouching in front of Kellach.

Her body jolted backward as a bolt of flame jetted out from the center of the amulet, missing the small wolf's nose by an inch. The little wolf yowled and huddled against the ground, covering its nose with its paws.

"It worked!" she cried, jumping up and down. "I did it!"

"Uh, Moyra?" Driskoll tugged on her arm. "We still have one small problem!"

The pony-sized wolf padded toward her, the growl low in its throat.

"Hah!" Moyra said. "I've got you this time." She pointed the amulet.

"Emalf," she said again. Flames shot out the amulet toward the large wolf, and seconds later, a thin trail of smoke rose from its left paw. Moyra smelled the stink of burning fur.

"Aiyee!" Moyra cried, throwing the branch at the large wolf. "Now get out of here!"

Driskoll and Kellach joined in, throwing their branches too. "Yeah! Get out!"

The wolves hopped to their feet and loped off. Moyra noticed with satisfaction that the big wolf was limping.

Moyra sat down on the back of the wagon. Her legs felt too wobbly to stand. She watched as Driskoll retrieved his sword from the trees. The battle with the winter wolves was finally over.

"So the rumors about the wolves are true," she said as the two boys joined her on the back of the wagon, both breathing hard.

"We'd better let everyone know," Driskoll said.

"We need to get out of here before they come back with the whole pack," Moyra said. She hopped off the wagon. Driskoll and Kellach nodded and wearily followed her down the road to town.

CHAPTER

7

They'd barely left the wagon when the snow started. The thick white flakes quickly blanketed the road again, clumping together in ever-growing drifts.

Kellach shot a worried look at the dark gray sky. "I don't like this," he said. "It's coming down awfully fast."

The snowflakes swirled in the air around them, making it hard to see the road home.

"By my estimate, it's still afternoon," Driskoll said. "Why is it so dark already?"

"Blizzard," Moyra said between clenched teeth. Her face already felt numb. The temperature had dropped, and it was so cold it hurt to breathe too deeply. She took shallow breaths and tried to think.

They trudged along in silence for a few minutes, slipping occasionally in the increasingly high drifts. The road was completely covered now. Moyra wondered if they were going the right way, but she didn't voice the thought.

"I can barely see a foot in front of my face," Driskoll protested. "And what if one of us gets lost? We wouldn't be able to tell."

"Let's stop for a minute," Kellach said. "We can barely see anyway."

Moyra glanced at him. There was a worried note in his voice.

They gathered near the shelter of a large oak tree. It wasn't much protection from the howling wind, but it was the best they could find.

"Do you think we should turn back and make for the ruins?" Moyra asked, wrapping her green scarf over her head.

Driskoll repressed a shudder. Spending the night at the ruins was not his idea of fun, Moyra knew.

"I think we should try to make it back to Curston," Kellach said. "Dad will no doubt send the watchers out in the blizzard looking for us if we're not home by the end of the day."

Moyra snapped her fingers. "I have an idea." She pulled out a rope.

Driskoll said, "But what good will a rope do us?"

Moyra grinned at him. "You'll see," she said.

"Good. It's long enough," she said and tied a length of the rope around her waist. "Here, Driskoll, you next, then Kellach."

At Driskoll's puzzled look, she explained, "This way, we'll be able to stay together no matter what. Even if we can't see."

"And if one of us is in trouble, we can tug on the rope," Kellach said. He tied the rope around his waist and picked up his knapsack. "If we hurry," he said bravely, "we can make it home in time for supper."

It was slow going, walking through mountains of snow. Moyra's feet felt like they were encased in lead. It was an effort to lift her feet enough to inch forward. Her nose hairs tingled with cold every time she took a breath.

At last, they saw the gates of Curston.

"Did we make it before curfew?" Driskoll said.

"They have to let us in," Moyra said. "The watchers might make me stay out here all night, but they'd never leave Torin's sons out in the cold."

"But if Dad finds out," Kellach said, "he won't let us leave the house ever again. I'd rather stay out here all night."

"We can't stay out here all night," Moyra said, shaking a wet sleeve. "My coat is soaked through." She looked at her friends. They were all cold and wet. "We'll freeze to death."

"If the wolves don't get us first," Driskoll said cheerfully.

"I'm only joking," he added quickly after seeing their faces.

Moyra looked at her friends for a minute, her mind racing.

The three of them had almost been locked out of Curston before. Some time later, Moyra overheard her father mention a secret entrance, the one the thieves guild used for their less than lawful activities. If she and the boys could sneak past the guild sentry, they would be home free.

About a hundred yards from the Westgate, Moyra spotted a large hedge sideling up to the stone wall. At least she thought it was the hedge. It was so snowy, she could barely see.

She glanced at Driskoll and Kellach, who were still staring mournfully at the closed gate.

"Here, put this on," she said. She reached into her pack, pulled out two thin strips of cloth, and handed them to Kellach. The old cloths she kept in her knapsack to use as bandages would have to do for blindfolds.

"Moyra, what is this all about?" Kellach asked. "Are you trying to kill us?"

She looked at him steadily. "I know a secret entrance. But if I show you, the thieves guild will have my hide. Still it's our only chance. So wear the blindfold, Kellach, and stop asking so many questions. We only have a few more minutes before your dad notices you two are gone."

To her relief, Kellach simply handed a blindfold to his brother and said, "Let's go."

After the boys tied on the blindfolds, Moyra led them to the hedge and prayed that she had overheard her father correctly.

"Wait here," she said, and she plunged into the scratchy branches. She reached out and was relieved to find a thick iron gate.

She went back through the hedge and, taking the boys by the hand, slowly and carefully led them to the small gate built into the wall.

She whispered, "Wait here," and quietly opened the door. It was barely tall enough for her to pass through without ducking her head.

She led the boys through the door and down a short tunnel. As she expected, the secret entrance opened directly into the alleyway of the Skinned Cat. It was time to get her friends out of Broken Town and send them home safe.

Moyra relaxed and stopped the boys by tugging on their hands. "It's safe to take the blindfolds off now," she whispered, "but we need to get out of Broken Town."

"You won't be going anywhere without talking to me first," a harsh voice said.

Someone put a heavy hand on Moyra's shoulder, and she whirled around with her fists raised, ready to attack.

CHAPTER

8

At the last minute, something stopped Moyra from landing a blow. As she turned, she caught a glimpse of a familiar face.

"Patch!" Moyra cried. She wrapped her arms around the elf and gave him a hug.

"Moyra, are you okay?" Kellach said in alarm. He still had his blindfold on and couldn't see what was happening.

"It's okay, Kellach. It's just my godfather." She stepped behind Kellach and untied his blindfold. "You remember Patch, right?" she said.

Kellach nodded as he removed the cloth covering his brother's eyes.

"You almost scared the life out of me," Moyra said to Patch. Her godfather was the owner of the Skinned Cat. The silver patch he wore over one eye gleamed. A dark-haired, horse-faced elf, he had lost an eye and half his ear in a battle that took place long ago. Moyra had tried asking him about it many times, but he refused to talk about it.

"And what are you doing in the alley of the Skinned Cat minutes before curfew?" her godfather asked, casting a sharp eye at the two boys.

Moyra's mind raced. If Patch realized she had brought the boys through the entrance, he could tell one of her father's friends, and she'd be done for.

"We-we're just playing a game, Patch," Moyra said hurriedly. "Hide and seek. But you're right, it's time for the boys to go home now," she added.

"A game," Patch repeated, raising one eyebrow and looking intently at Moyra. The corners of his mouth hinted at a smile. "Well, no harm done in a bit of gaming, as I always say."

Moyra's shoulders sagged with relief.

"I haven't seen that wizard friend of yours lately," Patch said casually.

Moyra's eyes narrowed. Patch didn't ask about Zendric to be polite. Something was going on.

"What have you heard?" Kellach said.

"Some are saying he's to blame for the cold," Patch said. "They're saying the weather isn't natural. They're saying it's the work of a wizard."

"I'm sure Zendric has n-nothing to do with it," Moyra stammered. "He's . . . gone."

"Ah, he is, is he?" Patch said, his finger absently tracing the scar on his face.

Driskoll jabbed his elbow into Moyra's side and hissed, "Why'd you have to tell him that?"

Patch cast a sharp glance at Driskoll. "I don't know what

rig you're running this time, my girl, but you'd best be careful. Those are Torin's sons. He's the captain of the watch, as you know very well."

The concern in her godfather's voice made Moyra pause. She couldn't tell him the truth, but she needed to tell him something to ease his mind a little. "Driskoll and Kellach are my friends, Patch," she said. "I'd never do anything to hurt them."

"See that you don't get hurt yourself, Moyra," he said. "There are strange things going on in Curston. Be careful."

"I will." Moyra promised. She was relieved that Patch had accepted her story, even if the look in his eye told her that he didn't necessarily believe it. "We should be going home. Good night, Patch," she said. She motioned to the boys, and together they hurried out the alley.

"That was a close one!" Driskoll said as soon as they had walked out of earshot.

Moyra looked back. Patch was still watching them. Driskoll didn't know how close of a call it had been.

▐ ▐ ▐ ▐ ▐

After saying a quick good-bye to her friends, Moyra ran home and reached her rickety porch, out of breath.

It was dusk, and she felt more tired than she'd ever felt in her life. Royma would probably be waiting at home with a long list of chores. And Moyra knew that Royma did not wait patiently.

Moyra was cold and hungry. She did not relish the thought of a few more hours of chores before she could crawl into bed. She yearned for a life with more ahead of it than just an unending list of work and not enough money.

The diamond would solve all their problems, Moyra knew. If only Zendric would return and give her his advice. She didn't want to sell it without talking to him, but she was running out of time.

She reached for the doorknob and twisted, pushing the creaky door open.

"I'm home!" she hollered.

"Get in here, girl," Royma called from the kitchen. "There are chores to be done."

By the time Moyra was finished carrying in the firewood and cleaning up after dinner, it was late.

She fell into bed, exhausted. She punched her pillow, trying to get comfortable. But she couldn't stop thinking about the diamond. Maybe she shouldn't wait for Zendric to come back before selling it. Her father would have sold it as soon as he found it without thinking twice.

But something felt wrong to Moyra. Her granny had always said that something too good to be true probably was. Moyra had the sinking feeling that the diamond would lead to trouble. Still she had no intention of letting it go, not now, when she was so close to having her dreams realized. Soon they would find Zendric, and everything would be solved.

With that thought in her mind, she fell into a restless sleep.

She had a horrible dream about a faceless stranger chasing her. In her dream, the blue diamond grew bigger and bigger. It rolled into Curston, plowing down everything in its path, including Moyra's friends and family.

She woke up, gasping. She sat up in bed, goose bumps breaking out over her body. It's just a dream, she thought to herself trying to calm down.

But what if it wasn't just a dream but a warning?

CHAPTER

9

The next morning, Moyra walked away from her mother's stand, her shoulders hunched against the cold. Today the merchants weren't rubbing their hands together in glee.

There were signs everywhere. Signs that read Out of Stock, No Food, and even a rude one that said: "I shall put a curse on the next person who asks."

Everyone was out of supplies. Even Royma had sold the last of her knitted scarves early that morning.

A crowd had gathered in the center of the square, waiting anxiously for the supply wagons. The magistrate, Pralthamus stood in front of a pair of angry dwarves.

"If the wagons don't arrive," one shouted, standing on the tips of her toes, "there will be nothing for my boys to eat!"

"We'll all be dead come next week, thanks to you!" squawked her fat friend. "What kind of leader are you?"

"Please, ladies, calm down," Pralthamus said, his face reddening with their mounting insults. "The ruling council and I are doing all we can to solve this crisis . . ."

"Like what?" the fat dwarf asked.

"Uh, I . . . ," Pralthamus bumbled. It was obvious he was as helpless as the rest of them.

Moyra wanted to talk to the boys about the diamond. She wanted to help her parents. But most of all, she wanted to find Zendric. She was searching the crowd and almost didn't see the pixie who brushed past her.

"Excuse me," the pixie said in a high sweet voice.

Moyra grabbed her. "Drop it," Moyra hissed, "or I'll squash you like a bug."

The pixie bit Moyra's hand, but Moyra held tight. Still holding fast to the squirming creature, Moyra looked around. She finally spotted the boys.

"Moyra!" Driskoll shouted, waving.

Kellach and Driskoll were only a few feet away but were held back by the flow of the crowd.

"Awfully heavy coin purse for a little girl," the pixie said, her eyes shining spitefully. "Especially for a Broken Town citizen."

"See my friends over there?" Moyra hissed, pointing toward Driskoll and Kellach. "Those boys are Torin's sons. You know Torin, the captain of the watch? Give it back, and they won't turn you over to the watchers. You know what happens to pixies in prison."

The pixie paled and reluctantly let go of the purse. It dropped with a thunk, and Moyra snatched it up, shoving it more securely into her pocket.

Moyra sagged with relief when she felt the gem thump against her ribs. She had been lucky this time. She lived in a thieves' paradise, so she should have known better. She'd practically been asking to get robbed.

Driskoll and Kellach finally managed to cross over to where Moyra stood fuming.

"What were you doing with that pixie?" Driskoll asked.

"None of your business," Moyra replied sharply.

Kellach glanced at her, his eyebrows raised, and she softened her voice. "She tried to pick my pocket, okay? But I let her go." Moyra sighed. "I felt sorry for her. I didn't want to see her end up in prison like . . . like my dad."

Driskoll stared at her, his brown eyes wide with compassion.

Moyra turned away. She didn't want anyone's pity.

Driskoll opened his mouth to speak, but he was distracted by the beat of a drum.

Two dwarves dressed in silver cloaks marched through the square playing bass drums almost as big as they were. One had a bushy brown beard, flecked with streaks of gray. The other seemed younger, wearing a white cap that hung down past his ears.

"Make way, make way for Fridjof!" the dwarves called.

Behind them came a silver and white caravan. It was enormous, like a cottage on wheels, complete with a skinny chimney and a door at the back. The caravan slowly threaded its way through the crowd.

Driving the caravan was a tall, thin man. His long, silvery blond hair flowed behind him. He was dressed richly in white ermine coat and boots, and he wore a fur hat upon his head. A

broad smile filled his face, which had a long scar running along one cheek.

Driskoll craned his neck as the townspeople crowded closer, trying to see. The caravan stopped in the middle of Main Square.

The man dressed in ermine hopped down with a graceful flourish.

Pralthamus stepped forward, accompanied by two watchers. "Who are you, stranger?"

There were mutters from the crowd.

"I am Fridjof, a simple merchant." The stranger gestured to the caravan. "I heard of the plight of your town and decided to journey here to ease the suffering of your people." He snapped his fingers. "Moli? Your assistance, please?"

The bearded dwarf set down his drum and rushed forward. Fridjof stood on one side of the caravan while Moli stood on the other. Moyra watched as the bearded dwarf reached up on his tiptoes to unhinge a silver hook on the broad side of the caravan. With a clatter, the entire top panel of the caravan swung down to become a makeshift table attached to the edge of the wagon by silver chains.

The younger dwarf scrambled through the door in the back of the caravan and began to set out the goods. Soon the table and all the space around it was piled high.

Moyra saw furs and warm woolen hats heaped up next to bushels filled with skeins of yarn. Sacks of grain leaned against bushels of bright red apples. The delightful smell of spices wafted through the crowd.

"Wonderful!" Pralthamus clapped his hands. Turning to face the crowd, he boomed, "Citizens of Curston, as always, in times of crisis, your magistrate will provide—"

But no one was interested in hearing the magistrate's speech. The crowd surged forward with a glad cry.

Fridjof held out a hand. "Patience, my friends, there is enough to go around. One at a time, please. My associates here will help you with your purchases."

Slowly a straggly line formed. Moyra and the boys wiggled their way to the front. "Gingerbread," Moyra said. "Do you smell gingerbread?" Her mouth watered.

The bearded dwarf motioned Moyra, Driskoll, and Kellach to come forward.

"You might be interested in these," he said as he began to unload a crate full of toys onto the makeshift table.

Moyra and the boys moved closer.

"This is a snow globe," Moli said, picking up a glass globe and shaking it. Miniature flakes covered the tiny town.

Driskoll laughed. "It looks just like a miniature Curston."

Moyra's eyes narrowed. The snow globe looked like the ones they had found at the ice palace.

The dwarf stooped down and began winding up small toys and setting them on the ground. Soon, a windup cat chased a windup mouse around and around.

"How do they work?" Driskoll asked Kellach. "Is it magic?"

"If there's magic," Kellach said, "it must be only a paltry amount. I think it works with tiny wheels. Did you see that he used a small key to turn them?"

Soon, there was a crowd of children gathered around. Moli went back into the caravan and returned with more windup toys, this time a group of life-size musicians. There were a dog playing a flute, a donkey playing a drum, and a cat playing a guitar. The tinny sound of music filled the air.

Next, the younger dwarf in the cap brought out an armful of dresses along with velvet cloaks. There were dresses that looked like they were made for a princess. Dresses the color of a rose, shot with silver threads. Dresses the color of the evening sky, trimmed with gold.

Moyra caught her breath, sick with greed. She wanted a dress like that. Just one dress. She watched as an elf girl scooped up several dresses and held them up for her mother. The elderly elf paid for the dresses without even blinking, Moyra thought enviously.

She turned away from the dresses and watched the crowd. It seemed as though everyone in Curston had money in his or her pockets. Everyone except her, that is.

Moyra spotted her mother, to one side of the line, scowling. She rushed over to her, visions of all the things she could buy swimming in her mind. She felt dizzy with all the choices.

"Mom, can I buy—" Moyra started to ask, but her mother's face already gave her the answer to her unfinished question.

"Moyra, you foolish girl," Royma said. "If business doesn't pick up, we won't be able to afford to eat. There's no money for trinkets." Royma said. She stared straight at Fridjof and cupped her hands around her mouth so that everyone could hear: "What do we merchants have to sell? Nothing, ever since the supply wagons stopped."

A reply burned in Moyra's throat, but she choked it down. It wasn't the time to tell her mother about the diamond.

"How did you manage to make it through the snowstorm anyway?" the gnome who sold patchwork caps asked Fridjof.

There were grumbles from several of the other merchants. Fridjof was competing against them, taking all their business away.

The stranger ignored their questions, and replied smoothly, "Not to worry, my friends. There will be another wagon here shortly to supply the merchants with their customary stock. But for now, I am happy to provide these items to you merchants at cost," he added with a smile.

The merchants rushed forward, all bargaining for the best deals for their stalls. Minutes later, Royma returned with her basket piled high with brightly colored yarn. "He's selling everything to merchants at half what we usually pay! He's practically giving the stuff away. I've got to get started knitting right away!" Royma headed off for her stall.

"And now," Fridjof boomed. "A gift for my friends in Curston."

Fridjof snapped his fingers, and the dwarves returned to the caravan. They came back a moment later, each carrying a large tray of gingerbread cut into all sorts of fantastical shapes. There were gingerbread owlbears, dragons, unicorns, and wolves along with the more traditional gingerbread men and women.

As the spicy smell wafted into the air, Moyra's stomach growled.

"Gingerbread!" Driskoll cried. Several people surged forward, elbowing their neighbors in their haste.

"With my compliments," Fridjof said. "There should be enough for everyone. Patience, please."

A cheer went up from the crowd.

When the noise died down, Fridjof said, "Thank you, my friends, for your warm welcome. There is one thing you can do for me in return. I am looking to purchase any rare or unusual items. I will pay well."

Moyra looked up quickly. Maybe she'd be able to sell the diamond. A stranger wouldn't ask any questions.

She moved forward, wanting to talk to Fridjof without Driskoll or Kellach noticing. She shot both of them a quick glance. They were gathered around the gingerbread tray.

The urge to sell the diamond grew. Without the money from its sale, Moyra would be left empty-handed, and unable to buy the gorgeous toys and clothes Fridjof and his helpers had brought.

She looked at Fridjof and met his strange pale eyes.

But then Moyra felt a tap on her shoulder.

"Hey, I got you an owlbear." Driskoll held out a cookie. "They're delicious. I just had two."

Kellach strolled up behind him, a half-eaten unicorn cookie hanging out of his mouth. "Did you notice that the tray never seemed to empty?" he said between chews.

"Really?" Driskoll said. "I'm going back for thirds, then!"

Moyra looked at Kellach, and they both laughed. She stuffed the owlbear's right leg in her mouth and let the cinnamon spice melt on her tongue. It was delicious, that was for sure.

Soon a second wagon arrived, heaped full of more supplies. Fridjof strode over to the wagon, and one of the horses shied, its hooves missing Fridjof by inches. The merchant said something in a low voice, and the horse immediately quieted.

Moyra looked over at the driver. He was a half-orc who wore a large triangular shaped hat.

She poked Kellach in the ribs. "Gods! Do you recognize that face?"

Kellach looked at her puzzled. "What?"

"That half-orc!" she whispered. "The driver? He looks like one of the figures in the snow globe at the palace. Come on, let's check it out."

"You're imagining things." Kellach replied. "I don't see any resemblance."

She glared at him.

He sighed. "Fine. I'll go with you, but I think you're hallucinating."

Moyra ignored his comment, and they started for the wagon.

Suddenly, Fridjof stepped in front of them. "May I help you, children?" he said.

"No, sir. We—we just want to see the horses." Kellach gave him an admiring glance. Morya saw Kellach's eyes widen at the sight of Fridjof's finery.

He looked at Kellach closely. "You are an apprentice to a wizard," Fridjof said.

Kellach's eyes narrowed. "How can you tell?"

Fridjof smiled. "Just a guess, I suppose. You look like the most intelligent one in this crowd."

Moyra watched as Kellach's chest swelled. Right along with his head, she thought, but she didn't say it aloud.

"You guessed correctly," he said proudly. "I am apprenticed to Zendric."

Fridjof smiled broadly, and his eyes darted through the crowd. "Ah, Zendric. Is he still alive? Where is he?"

"He's . . . out of town," Kellach said.

Fridjof's smile disappeared.

"Do you know Zendric?" Moyra asked.

But Fridjof ignored her. "Perhaps you have something of Zendric's to sell, young man?" Fridjof continued.

"No, sir," Kellach replied.

"No matter," Fridjof said smoothly. "But please let me know if you hear of anything. I'm sure a bright lad like you has many friends in this town. I would appreciate the assistance."

Kellach smiled. "I would be happy to help you, sir," he said eagerly. Moyra felt like rolling her eyes.

Fridjof's blue eyes gleamed as he turned to Moyra. "And you, young lady, perhaps you have something you wish to sell?"

It seemed to Moyra that his eyes could see right through her pocket to the diamond concealed inside her jacket. The jewel seemed to grow heavier, and her hand twitched, wanting to draw it out, wanting to show it. This was her chance! All her problems would be solved right there. But something held her back. She looked up into Fridjof's icy eyes and shook her head, clearing the strange lethargy that had overtaken her.

"No, no, I don't," Moyra said, avoiding those strange eyes.

"No? If you find anything interesting, you know where to find me." Fridjof said.

Moyra couldn't tear her eyes from the jagged scar running down his face. She stood in front of the merchant, speechless, until Kellach tugged on her hand and led her away.

"Are you okay?" Kellach asked her.

"I'm fine," Moyra said, "but that guy gives me the creeps."

"He seemed nice," Kellach protested. "But I wonder why he asked you if you had anything to sell." What Kellach didn't say was that Moyra and her mother were unlikely to have anything of value to sell.

Moyra scrambled for an answer. "My dad is a thief, Kellach," she said. "Maybe he was looking to buy something from him."

Kellach gave her a concerned look but changed the subject.

"Come on, let's go back to my house. I need to translate that clue we found inside the marble lion."

Moyra nodded. But as they walked to Kellach's home in the Phoenix Quarter, she felt a draft, as if an icy hand was at her back.

CHAPTER

10

"The magistrate is planning an ice-skating party!" Driskoll burst through the front door of his house an hour later.

Moyra and Kellach looked up from their seats at the table. Kellach had been trying to translate the clue they had found inside the lion. But so far he'd deciphered only the first word.

"Ice skating?" Kellach said.

"Yes," Driskoll said. "To celebrate Fridjof's arrival. Fridjof brought a whole box of boots with blades attached. He told the magistrate he'd loan them out for free."

"Where are we going to skate?" Moyra asked skeptically.

"The river is frozen solid. Fridjof says he'll teach everyone how to do it. They ice-skate all the time where he's from," Driskoll said.

"Yes, where exactly is he from?" Moyra asked.

Driskoll ignored her. "Do you want to go? Dad has to work, but he said it's okay if we go."

Kellach and Moyra looked at each other in silence.

"I know we need to translate the amulet message," Driskoll said. "But it will be so fun. And since Curston might not see snow ever again, it could be a once-in-a-lifetime opportunity!"

Kellach looked at Moyra. "Why not? The whole town's bound to be there. I want to talk to Fridjof anyway."

"No!" Moyra said, "We shouldn't say anything to him about the amulets."

"I know better than that," Kellach said. "I just want to hear about his travels." He looked at Moyra curiously.

She shook her head. "Sorry. I'm just being paranoid."

Driskoll laughed as he danced out the door. "You can say that again!"

The river flowed just outside the outskirts of Curston, moving along the northern edge of the city walls. The wagons filled with townspeople, with Fridjof's silver and white caravan in the lead, stopped near a bend in the river, close to a grove of tall pines. The dwarves who worked for Fridjof gathered firewood for a bonfire. The townspeople joined in the hunt for wood and soon, there were small fires blazing away back from the river. Within minutes, a large pot was set over one of the fires. The smell of sweet spiced cider drifted over to where Driskoll, Kellach, and Moyra stood.

A small child looked up and pointed at the tall white spires in the distance. "What's that?" he asked.

A murmur went up from the crowd. A sense of unease permeated the air, blotting out the festive atmosphere.

"It's my new home," Fridjof said smoothly. "Now, let's skate."

Soon everyone was laughing and joking as parents found skates for their children. The frozen river filled with people skating shakily. Fridjof glided among them, offering encouragement and pointers.

Driskoll immediately strapped on a pair of skates and, wobbling wildly, sped off. Kellach waited patiently while Moyra put on her skates.

"I've never been skating before," she said. "I'm not really sure how to do it." She looked down at her skates doubtfully.

"It's easy. I'll teach you. Take my hand, and I'll help you until you get the hang of it." Kellach said.

They went out onto the ice. After a few shaky strokes, Moyra could skate without Kellach's help. In no time, she was whizzing around the ice.

Some of the boys started a game of crack-the-whip. Moyra skated up to the end of the line and joined hands with Driskoll. As the line snaked around, Moyra felt as if her skates weren't touching the ground.

"It's like flying!" she said breathlessly. She let go of Driskoll's hand and went spinning around, crashing into Kellach.

"Ow," she moaned, as she wobbled to her feet. "That part wasn't as fun. I think I'm thirsty for some hot cider."

"Hot cider sounds good to me," Kellach said.

"Driskoll," Moyra called out as he skated past her. "Fridjof brought hot cider for the party, but it's going fast. We're going to get some before it's all gone. Want some?"

"No, thanks. I'm staying on the ice." Driskoll skidded to a

stop beside her. His cheeks were red from excitement and cold. He paused only for a moment to catch his breath before skating off.

"Driskoll, passing up food?" Kellach said. "I don't believe it! He must be having fun."

Moyra and Kellach stayed by the shore and watched him skate around. Moyra cupped the hot cider around her hands to warm them. It wasn't quite as good as hot chocolate, but she couldn't complain. At least it was hot. And Fridjof promised that the next supply wagons would be filled to the brim with chocolate. She could hardly wait.

She looked around at all the laughing people. She could forget about her problems on a day like this.

"Your brother has certainly taken to ice skating," a voice said.

They turned. It was Fridjof standing to their right, at the edge of the ice. Moyra noticed that even Fridjof's skates were white and trimmed with ermine instead of the more practical black leather ones the rest of the skaters wore.

"He's skated before," Kellach replied politely. "We both have."

To Moyra he added, "Zendric froze the river once and took us for a lesson, but only for an hour."

"Zendric?" Fridjof smiled. "I see. But why would he take Driskoll?" He leaned down closer to Kellach.

Kellach shrugged. "Driskoll is a . . . a good friend of Zendric's too."

Fridjof didn't reply but, instead, stared speculatively at Driskoll.

Moyra fiddled with her mittens as Fridjof stood there, watching, without saying anything. As they watched, Driskoll disappeared around the bend.

"Driskoll!" Kellach called, but there was no answer from his brother.

"I'll go look after him. It's not safe to wander off from the group," Fridjof said and skated off in the direction Driskoll had headed.

Suddenly, there was a loud cracking noise as the ice gave under the weight of a heavy object, somewhere along the river.

Moyra heard a faint cry for help.

"Driskoll!" Moyra and Kellach cried. They tightened their ice skates and launched themselves across the river. They skated downstream, following the shoreline in the direction of the cry.

As they rounded the bend in the river, they saw Fridjof carrying the limp body of Driskoll.

"Quickly, get blankets," Fridjof said. "Tell someone to get the caravan ready. We have to get him back to Curston and out of these wet clothes right away."

"What happened?" Kellach said.

"Let's get him near the fire first," Fridjof said, panting a little as he skated back to the rest of the group. He slid off the ice and onto the snow, and still wearing his skates, he carried Driskoll near the fire. Driskoll was soaking wet and shivering.

"The ice wasn't completely frozen," Fridjof explained. "He was skating very fast and not paying attention. I had almost caught up to him when the ice gave way, and he went into the river."

Moyra stared at him. The river water had to be ice cold, but Fridjof's teeth didn't even chatter. What was even more strange, there wasn't a trace of water on Fridjof.

Royma came up as Fridjof was explaining what happened. "You're a hero!" she exclaimed. "Driskoll is lucky you were there."

Kellach looked up at the merchant, tears dotting the corner of his eyes. "You saved my brother."

Royma said, "Don't just stand there gawking, Moyra. Fetch Driskoll's father. And the cleric."

"There's no need," Fridjof interrupted. "My horses have been harnessed, and my caravan is ready. It will be faster to take him to the cleric's for healing instead of waiting. We'll be in Curston in no time. There are some old clothes and furs in the back. They'll keep him warm."

Moyra loitered outside the back of the wagon while Royma and Kellach changed Driskoll out of his sodden clothes.

When her mother emerged, Moyra asked, "Can we ride back to Curston with them?"

Royma glanced at Fridjof. "I'm not sure that would be a good idea."

"Nonsense." Fridjof said as he turned to Moyra's mother with a charming smile. "I'm afraid I don't know the way to the cleric's. I would appreciate your company." Fridjof opened the back door of the caravan. "Moyra, why don't you ride in the back with Driskoll and Kellach. And Royma, my dear, perhaps you would be so kind as to ride up front with me and"—Fridjof extended his hand—"show me the way."

Moyra watched in fascinated horror as Fridjof helped her mother into the front seat of the wagon. Her mother slipped a bit as she climbed up onto the high seat and she giggled. Moyra stared at her mother. She'd never heard her mother giggle.

Moyra climbed in the back of the caravan. Covered with light wooden panels and lit with dangling lanterns, the walls fairly glowed. A thick silver and blue oriental carpet covered the floor. At the far end of the caravan, tucked into an alcove was a small bunk. There, Driskoll lay, swaddled in blankets and furs. His face was white, and his eyes were closed.

Kellach sat on the bunk next to his brother, looking worried.

"Has he said anything?" Moyra asked.

"No. Not yet," Kellach replied.

Moyra looked around, wanting to kick a wall. "He *has* to be all right."

"I wish Zendric were here," Kellach said softly. "He'd know what to do."

"Do you think it's weird that Fridjof went after Driskoll just before he fell through the ice?" Moyra asked. "It's almost as if he knew Driskoll would fall in." Somewhere in the back of her mind, she couldn't help thinking Fridjof had something to do with Driskoll's accident.

Kellach scoffed. "What's your problem, Moyra? You're being paranoid. Fridjof *saved* Driskoll."

A while later, they felt the caravan slowing down. It seemed like it had taken hours to reach Curston, but Moyra knew it wasn't that long.

She looked out the small oval window. She recognized

Latislav's house, and the caravan came to a stop. Moyra threw open the caravan's doors and hopped out. Kellach stayed with his brother.

Royma jumped from the driver's seat and went to the cleric's front door. She pounded on it until he answered. They told the Latislav what had happened, and he rushed to the back of the caravan to examine Driskoll, shooing them all away, with the exception of Kellach, who refused to leave his brother's side.

Moyra paced back and forth while Fridjof and her mother conversed in low voices.

At last, Latislav came out and said, "It looks like he'll recover, but he needs to rest. It's that lump on his head that worries me."

"What do you mean?" Moyra asked. Fridjof hadn't mentioned a lump on Driskoll's head.

Fridjof stepped forward and said, "Perhaps the young man hit his head on a log or stone. I did see several near the spot where he fell in."

Latislav nodded. "That's probable," he said. "Someone needs to check on him while he sleeps. If he doesn't wake up in a few hours, send word."

"He's awake," Kellach called from the door of the caravan. "He says his head hurts and he's hungry."

They all crowded into the caravan and huddled around the small bunk.

"Thank you for saving me, sir," Driskoll said, looking up at Fridjof. His voice sounded hoarse.

"What happened, Dris?" Moyra leaned in closer. "Do you remember?"

Driskoll closed his eyes. "I was having so much fun skating that I didn't notice how far I had gone . . . I turned the bend and then . . ." He opened his eyes and trained them on Fridjof. "The next thing I remember you were pulling me out of the icy water. Thank you so much. If you hadn't arrived when you did . . . "

"Yes, thank you!" Kellach said, seizing Fridjof's hand and shaking it repeatedly.

Moyra felt ashamed of her suspicions. The diamond *was* making her paranoid.

CHAPTER

11

The next afternoon, the three kids sat in Driskoll and Kellach's room. Driskoll had spent the morning sleeping, but by early afternoon, he was so bored that they could hardly keep him from bouncing out of bed. Torin had finally permitted Driskoll to get up and change into his clothing, but only after Moyra and Kellach promised repeatedly to watch over him.

Kellach held the amulet's clue in his hand. He had finished translating the Elvish words the night before. But even translated, the message was still a mystery.

"We can't give up," Moyra said. "I have a feeling it will lead us to another amulet. And finding the other amulets may help us find Zendric. Read it again."

"Where the dragonflies, you shall find fire in the dragon's breath," Kellach repeated.

"It doesn't make any sense!" Driskoll said, flopping down onto his bed. He was still a little pale, but otherwise it seemed he had completely recovered from his dunking in the river. "Dragonflies? We're looking for bugs in the middle of winter?"

"Dragonflies, dragonflies," Kellach muttered as he paced the room. "Maybe it's not referring to an insect. Maybe it's two words. Dragon," Kellach paused. "Flies."

Moyra nodded. "So where do dragons fly around here? I can't think of anything like that in the ruins."

"What about in Curston?" Kellach asked without looking up.

Driskoll took in a quick breath and sat up. "I've got it! The Flying Dragon!"

The Flying Dragon was one of the many inns on Visitor Street where wealthier travelers stopped to rest from a long journey. Moyra had never stayed there although she had seen it. The Flying Dragon was an inn catering to the rich.

"Yes!" Moyra's hand shot in the air. "That must be it! Let's go!"

■ ▮ ▊ ▮ ▮

A half an hour later, Kellach, Driskoll, and Moyra stood in front of the inn.

"What now?" Driskoll asked.

Moyra bit her lip. "Maybe it's in a dragon. Look for anything unusual. Something that could conceal an amulet."

Kellach looked at the Flying Dragon in dismay. There had to be over a hundred dragons decorating the exterior of the inn. There were stone dragons perched in each corner of the roof.

There were dragons carved into the front door. There was even a dragon fountain in the courtyard.

"It could be any one of these!" Kellach said. "There are dragons all over the place."

Moyra slumped her shoulders. "You're right. Read the clue again. Maybe we missed something."

"Where the dragon flies, you shall find fire in the dragon's breath," Kellach said.

"Dragon's breath?" Driskoll repeated. "Dragon's breath is hot, right? Where is there heat in an inn?"

"The kitchen!" Moyra said.

They raced to the back door, which led to the kitchen, but stopped in the doorway when they realized they'd have to have a reason to enter.

"The cook won't let three strange children search the cupboards," Moyra pointed out. She was used to suspicion since she was the daughter of a well-known thief.

They huddled outside the kitchen door and tried to decide what to do next.

"Wait a minute!" Kellach said. "I think I translated it wrong. I thought it said dragon's breath because that would kind of make sense. But I was wrong. It says 'dragon words,'"

Driskoll looked at Moyra.

"The library!" they cried.

Off the main room of the inn was an alcove lined with the huge oak bookcases. The bookcase frames were carved with dragons, and hundreds of books filled the shelves.

"If anyone asks, we can say that Zendric sent us to look for a book," Moyra suggested. They returned to the front of the building and passed through the oak doors. Once inside, they casually waved to the innkeeper.

The innkeeper scowled at them, but didn't say anything. Thelonius was known as a grumpy old man, and the children knew they had only a few minutes before he'd come over to shoo them away. Fortunately, the inn was crowded and Thelonius was busy serving his guests cider and hot stew.

Driskoll drew in an appreciative breath. "It smells delicious."

"We just ate. How can you be hungry again?" Kellach said.

Driskoll shrugged. "What should we look for?"

"Look for anything unusual," Kellach said.

They turned their attention to the bookshelves. The books were piled almost to the ceiling, and several columns looked in danger of toppling over if anyone breathed too hard.

Moyra stepped over a stack of old scrolls and looked closely at the bookshelf. "Look, the bookends. They're dragons. Silver dragons."

Driskoll picked one up. "It seems too light to be made of solid silver."

He turned it over. "There's an opening in the bottom." He shook it gently and a small item wrapped in cloth fell out.

"This is it. Look, there's something written on the cloth. It says Knights of the Silver Dragon." Driskoll unfolded the cloth carefully. Inside was a dark black stone, just like the one they'd found in the lion.

"That's it! Another fire amulet!" Moyra said.

"Kellach, you should hold onto it." Driskoll handed the amulet to his older brother. "You're the oldest and the senior Knight in Zendric's absence."

"No, you found it, Driskoll, you keep it," Kellach said.

Driskoll began wrapping the amulet back in the cloth. "Wait! I think I found another clue. It's written on the other side of the cloth." He held up the cloth. "How strange. This one's in common language."

Kellach leaned over his brother's shoulder. "'Round and round, a shape without end, you will find this fire with a friend.'" He looked at Moyra. "This is Zendric's handwriting!"

"I knew it. That means we're on the right track."

"'You will find this fire with a friend,'" Driskoll repeated. He looked up. "Maybe that means we'll find the next amulet with Zendric!"

Footsteps came up behind them.

Kellach glanced over his shoulder. "Quick! Hide the cloth. Here comes the innkeeper."

"Hello, children," Thelonius said. His dark eyebrows drew together. "May I help you with something?"

"We-we just wanted to look at the books," Driskoll said as Kellach discreetly placed the silver dragon bookend back on the shelf.

"I don't allow children to touch my books," Thelonius snapped. "These books are very precious. I think it's time you left."

He stood there, obviously waiting for them to go.

"What's this?" Driskoll asked. He pointed to a faint mark on the wall.

"I don't see anything," Thelonius said quickly.

"Right here." Driskoll touched a symbol painted on the wall, just above the baseboard. "It looks like a silver dragon. I think I saw something like it in Zendric's—"

"Get your grubby hands off my walls!" Thelonius shouted. "I tried doing this the easy way, but I see children like you cannot be trusted. Now get out." He pointed toward the front door.

"Sorry," Driskoll said, holding his hands up defensively. "I didn't mean—"

"Come on, Driskoll," Moyra said, pulling him by the arm. "There's no point arguing. Let's go before he calls the watch." Kellach followed her and Driskoll to the exit.

"That man's crazy!" Driskoll said as they walked down Visitor Street back toward Main Square.

"I think he might know something about Zendric's disappearance," Moyra said.

Driskoll looked up at her. "Why do you say that?"

"Didn't you notice that he asked us to leave right after you mentioned Zendric? I think we should sneak back in there and have another look around."

"I don't know," Kellach said. "Zendric always said that anyone who loves books can't be all bad."

"Do you have a better idea?" Moyra said.

Kellach and Driskoll shook their heads.

Kellach said, "We'll have to do it later. Dad wants us home for dinner." Kellach shrugged. "I think Driskoll's accident really scared him. He wants to meet us for every meal and he made us promise to stay within the city walls, at least until the weather clears. He's been hanging over us like a hawk."

"That's okay," Moyra said. "I have to help my mom close up the stall. She'll be furious if I show up late."

The children agreed to meet at the marketplace the next day. They departed, each worried about the fate of their friend Zendric.

CHAPTER

12

When Moyra arrived at her mother's stall, she was surprised to see Fridjof there. Royma was sitting in a chair, knitting.

Moyra watched in amazement as the merchant took Royma's hand and kissed it lingeringly. Nobody was allowed to interrupt when Royma was knitting. Moyra waited for her the explosion, but it never came. Instead, Royma smiled up at Fridjof.

Moyra's jaw dropped. Her mother couldn't be falling for his smooth charm, could she?

"It's such a shame that you have to work so hard, my dear," Fridjof said. "If only I'd met you before . . ." His voice trailed off, but he continued to gaze meaningfully into Royma's eyes.

Moyra was amazed to see her mother blush a becoming pink.

"We won't be working so hard once my Dad is out," Moyra said. Her mother's lips tightened at the mention of her husband.

"Hello, my child." Fridjof looked up at her. Moyra felt as if a cold wind had whistled past her ears. She was chilled to the bone, despite several layers of old clothes.

"Oh, Fridjof, darling," Royma said, flustered. "You remember my daughter, Moyra."

"Certainly." Fridjof flashed an icy smile. "I hope your friend Driskoll has recovered from his accident."

Moyra's eyes narrowed. "Don't you have something you should be doing? Some sales to make?"

"My associates are taking care of business. Right now, my only piece of business,"—he lifted Royma's hand and kissed it—"is to give your beautiful mother a much needed treat."

Royma tittered. "Oh, Fridjof. You're so silly." Moyra turned to her daughter. "Fridjof's offered to treat me to a hot cup of cider. We were waiting here for you so you could watch the stall until we return."

Moyra felt desperation rise in her chest. She had never seen her mother act so girlishly. Her mother was falling for Fridjof!

Maybe her mom was just being friendly with Fridjof because he seemed to be wealthy. If she sold the diamond, maybe the money would make Royma happy, and she'd stop smiling at Fridjof.

Moyra took a deep breath. She ignored the unease snaking down her back. "You said you bought unusual items? Would you be interested, uh, in a rare gem?"

"Let me see it," he commanded.

"I don't have anything to show you. I was wondering if you bought gems . . . for a friend."

"Yes, yes." Fridjof could scarcely contain his interest. "Tell me more about this gem. What does it look like? Is it an emerald? A ruby? A diamond? A particularly large diamond? I'd pay you well." Fridjof's long thin fingers dug into her arm.

Royma laughed, and Fridjof loosened his grip. "Don't pay her any mind, Fridjof. She's just trying to get attention. Moyra doesn't have a diamond. If she did I'd know about it."

Royma held out her knitting needles to Moyra. "Now, take over for me."

Moyra groaned, but she obeyed her mother and took the knitting needles Royma handed her.

"I'll be back in a few minutes. Be good!" Royma waved and took Fridjof's arm in an overly familiar way.

Moyra watched them walk away. Royma laughed and smiled as they walked along. Moyra gritted her teeth.

She picked up the needles and began knitting furiously. The needles clacked together as she angrily tossed the yarn over and under her stitches.

How could her mother forget about her husband, Moyra's father, Breddo, who languished in prison? How could she be fooled by a few greasy compliments and crooked smiles?

Moyra scoffed. And she had almost sold her priceless diamond to that slimy wife stealer! Well, never again! She'd find some other way to dispense with her diamond.

As she saw Royma hurrying back to the stall, Moyra looked down at her work and grimaced. The needles kept tangling up in the yarn. "By Harrid's horn!" she said. "I'm hopeless at this knitting stuff."

"I'll take that now," Royma said.

Moyra handed the needles to her mother guiltily. The scarf was now a jumbled snarl of yarn.

"What in the world have you done?" Royma screeched. "This is terrible work, even for you. You've been acting so strangely lately." Royma pulled at the yarn, unraveling it as best she could. "What was that about a diamond earlier? Fridjof kept asking me about it as we drank our cider. It ruined our entire outing."

Royma looked at her daughter, with one eyebrow raised. "I trust that if you had something valuable to sell, you would tell me. You wouldn't hoard it like your father, right?"

"Of course, Mom." Moyra scowled. "I was just pretending. Trying to get Fridjof's attention, like you said." She reached out for the knitted mess. "Here, I'll help untangle it."

"You've helped enough," Royma said sharply, turning away from her daughter. "I'll take care of this. Just go."

That was a first, Moyra thought sourly. Her mother must really want to get rid of her. "Fine. I'm going home." But she really had something else in mind.

She ran off down the row of tents. She needed to hide the diamond. She felt it was no longer safe with her now that Royma suspected she had something valuable to sell.

The atmosphere of the market was glum. A huge troll walked next to Moyra, and she heard his stomach growl. There would be more growling bellies soon if the cold snap didn't end. Moyra moved away from the troll. They rarely ate humans anymore, but why tempt fate?

Her mind raced trying to think of the best hiding place. The safest place she knew was Zendric's tower.

She noticed one of the dwarves who worked for Fridjof loitering on the corner. She thought it was odd that he was hanging about when Fridjof would need his help with the supply wagon. She had the strange feeling he was following her. Maybe Fridjof told him what she'd said about the diamond. Moyra sighed. Everybody in Curston wanted a piece of her treasure!

"It's now or never," she whispered to herself and took off from Main Square at a sedate pace. She would hide the diamond, but she would head toward Broken Town first to see if the dwarf followed her.

The dwarf was behind her, she could tell. She could smell the smoke from his pipe.

"I'll lose him in Broken Town for sure." Moyra knew every shortcut and hiding place in Broken Town. Moyra wanted to run, but forced herself to stay at a slow walk.

She casually turned her head and pretended to wave at a startled elderly elf. She scanned the crowd. There was the dwarf, pretending to study a sign.

When the dwarf looked the other way, Moyra ducked into an alley and threaded her way to the back entrance of the Skinned Cat.

As she entered, she almost stepped on a tipsy pixie and nearly got stomped by a moody half-orc. The Skinned Cat was full to the brim that day. She weaved her way through the crowd. She saw Patch at the bar and gave him a cheery wave, and then she slipped out the front door.

Moyra looked back and forth down the narrow street and felt a breath she didn't even know she was holding whoosh out her lungs.

There was no sign of the dwarf. She'd lost him. She broke into a run and headed straight for Zendric's tower. As she ran along, little puffs of her breath hung in the air.

She opened the tower door, hoping against hope to see her friend Zendric. But the tower was deserted.

She quickly moved to the bookshelf and pulled out one of Zendric's thick books. She stuffed her coin purse, which contained the diamond, in the empty space and replaced the tome. There. Now, at least her diamond was safe.

She meandered home, lost in thought. After they found Zendric, she would sell the diamond. But not to Fridjof. To some other merchant, one who didn't have his sights set on breaking up her family.

Then her mother wouldn't have to worry so much, and she'd forget about Fridjof. They could finally get Moyra's father out of prison. And maybe, if there were enough money left over, Moyra could buy a new dress. A dress like the ones Fridjof sold.

Snow fell in quick little bursts, covering Broken Town and disguising the worst of its faults. It looked almost pretty, but Moyra knew that no one would live in Broken Town unless they had to.

Her feet took her to her doorstep before she knew it. She opened the front door. The house was dark and cold. She headed for the hearth to light a fire when something stopped her cold.

Moyra's home was small, but Royma always kept it completely spotless. Which is why Moyra noticed a tiny drop of water pooled near the hearth.

A chill crept up Moyra's spine. Someone had been in her house.

CHAPTER

13

Moyra rushed around the small cottage. She checked the windows, but they were closed and locked just as always.

She checked the door for any sign of a break-in. Nothing. She looked in the oak cupboard where Royma kept their nicest linens and where Breddo sometimes stashed his loot.

Nothing was missing, nothing was out of place.

Then she stepped into the kitchen.

In the center of the tiny room, was an elaborately carved cedar chest, similar to the ones she'd seen Fridjof's dwarves carry, only smaller.

Just the size for a girl Moyra's age.

Moyra studied the chest for a moment, looking for clues. She didn't want to open the chest and be overcome by a spell. She should get Kellach and Driskoll, she thought. But somehow she knew she didn't want to ask for Kellach's help. Whatever was in the chest was for her eyes only.

She took a deep breath and lifted the lid.

A velvet dress and matching jacket lay nestled in the bottom of the chest. She grasped the dress by the shoulders and held it up. It was the most beautiful thing she'd ever seen.

She ran her hand over the soft velvet. It was the color of dusk, a pale purple, and it was trimmed with white ermine fur.

Moyra frantically glanced at the door. She knew her mother would be at the market for at least another half hour. She didn't want Royma to see the dress. Royma would probably sell it instead of letting Moyra keep it.

Quickly she slipped off her clothes, and stepped into the dress. It felt like stepping into a cloud. Dozens of tiny pearl buttons lined the bodice. Moyra's fingers fumbled as she fastened them. She couldn't believe it but the dress fit her perfectly. She slipped on the short jacket. Its soft, fur-trimmed collar and sleeves tickled her skin.

She went to their only mirror, which was really a bit of mirrorstone that Kellach had given her.

The neckline was gathered in a pretty ruffle that scooped just under her collarbone. The velvet skirt fell to her ankles. White fur brushed against the tops of her shoes.

Moyra thought that the dress made her, a thief of Broken Town, look as elegant as royalty. She twirled around, the dress puffing out as she spun. For the first time in her life, she felt like a princess.

She went back to the mirror and swept into a low curtsy like she'd seen the well-born ladies of Curston do. And then she frowned. Peeking out from underneath her dress were her heavy black boots. They didn't match her dress, she thought anxiously.

Maybe they wouldn't show from beneath the hem.

Or maybe, just maybe, the chest wasn't empty yet.

She hurried back to the cedar box and lifted the lid again. As if by magic, it seemed a few more items had appeared. She probably hadn't noticed them in her excitement, Moyra reasoned. She found a pair of soft leather slippers, a necklace made with a sparkling green stone, a matching hair clip, and even a small vial of perfume.

The smile faded from Moyra's face. Those wonderful things couldn't be for her. She began to lower the lid, and then she noticed one more thing. A note.

She picked up the yellowed parchment and read:

My dearest Moyra,

It has been a joy to make the acquaintance of you and your wonderful mother. Please accept this gift as a token of my friendship, with my deepest compliments.

Ever yours,
Fridjof

She crumbled the note into a ball. The dress was a bribe. He thought he'd fool her with expensive presents. He wanted her to like him so he could walk away with her mother.

She'd wear the dress, all right. But only to show that sleazy merchant that he couldn't buy her off.

Moyra would never let Fridjof steal her mother, not for all the money in the world.

CHAPTER

14

The next morning, the sky was once again dark, and snow-flakes swirled in the air. Moyra hoped against hope that there wasn't another storm on its way. Kellach and Driskoll were supposed to meet her at Royma's stall. She continued to study the sky as she made her way to the marketplace.

There were people, standing in line everywhere, already waiting for the market to open, but no sign of Driskoll or Kellach.

Moyra's eyes gleamed. There was time to earn a little money before her friends arrived. She looked around for some likely targets.

Fifteen minutes later, Moyra was crouched at the mouth of an alleyway, playing dice with an elderly centaur, the rich elf from the bakery, and Grellen, a half-orc with more money than sense.

Out of the corner of her eye, Moyra saw Kellach and Driskoll. They were headed for her mother's stall, obviously looking for Moyra.

She kept one eye on the boys and the other on the dice. She couldn't be distracted right now. Money was on the line, money she couldn't afford to lose. She hoped that a rogue's luck was with her that day. She tossed the dice and easily won. She was scooping her winnings up with one hand when a beefy paw stopped her.

"You're cheating," Grellen bellowed.

Moyra sighed. She hadn't cheated. Moyra had a way with the dice, and that was all.

"Moyra, I'm not leaving until I get my money back," the half-orc cried.

"Shh! Everyone will hear you," Moyra said, looking around to see if they'd been observed. She had promised her mom no more gambling, but they were almost out of food, and what else could she do?

Moyra glared at Grellen. "Do you want everyone to know you were beaten by me?"

Kellach and Driskoll had heard Grellen shouting her name and came running down the alley.

"Moyra, are you okay?" Driskoll yelled.

Kellach took in the scene with a glance. "Moyra, you know what my dad said the last time he caught you gambling."

"His father, Torin, captain of the watch," she reminded Grellen calmly. Grellen suddenly looked uncertain, and his grasp on her arm loosened.

Moyra snatched up the money and bolted.

"Run!" she told Kellach and Driskoll. They had no choice but to follow her.

"Split up, you dolts," she said.

Out of the corner of her eye, she saw a flash of Driskoll's brown hair as they headed back to the market. She heard Grellen's heavy footsteps pounding behind her. She sped up and veered for Broken Town.

She turned the corner, out of breath. She didn't hear Grellen, so she slowed to a walk. Grellen was mild mannered, for a half-orc. He would have forgotten his anger by now. Moyra decided it was safe to head back to Main Square.

She strolled back toward her mother's stall, feeling pleased with herself. She counted her winnings in the shadows of the Cathedral of St. Cuthbert. Not bad for a day's work.

"Quite a little brouhaha," Fridjof said. "I'm sure your mother would be interested in your activities."

Moyra could have sworn no one was following her. How had he found her?

"I didn't cheat," she said stubbornly. "It's my money."

"You could have much more money than that," Fridjof said.

"I don't know what you're talking about," Moyra replied. What did he mean? If he married her mother, would her family be rich? Or—Moyra gulped—did he know she had the diamond?

Fridjof's blue eyes met hers, and Moyra felt a chill to her very soul. His eyes were as clear and as cold as a frozen lake.

To her relief, Driskoll and Kellach came racing up to them.

"Excuse us, sir," Kellach said, bowing politely, "but we are late for an appointment with my father."

Kellach took Moyra by the arm, and they slowly walked away with Driskoll tagging at their heels.

Moyra was relieved that Fridjof didn't try to stop them. She couldn't resist the temptation to look back. Fridjof had not stirred from the spot they had left him. He stood there with a faint smile upon his face.

Once they were out of earshot, Kellach asked, "What was going on, Moyra? I didn't like the way you were looking at him. Is everything all right?"

"I'm fine, Kellach," Moyra said. "It was nothing."

"Then why did you look so scared?" Driskoll asked.

"I thought I was going to get into trouble for gambling. Fridjof knows my mom and the other merchants at the market." Moyra thought the lie didn't even sound convincing to her own ears. She didn't like lying to her friends, but she wasn't ready to tell them her secret yet.

"There are a lot of people here this morning," Driskoll said in a low voice. "What's going on?'"

Moyra looked around. He was right. There were townspeople everywhere. And they looked like they were in an angry mood. They thronged together in clumps, making it difficult to pass.

"Dad said that there still isn't enough food to go around," Kellach said. "Fridjof promised there would be another set of supply wagons. But they still haven't arrived. Everyone is waiting."

As if on cue, Fridjof stepped through the crowd. He cleared his throat and bellowed, "My friends, I am sorry to have to bring you bad news. I had offered my hospitality to Curston willingly, and I had hoped to receive something valuable in return." Moyra felt as if Fridjof's eyes were boring into her.

"After days of waiting, I'm afraid I was unable to find what I was looking for," the merchant continued bellowing. "Now I have other business to attend to, and I must leave your fair city before the full moon."

"But you can't leave now!" a half-orc hollered. "Where will we get our supplies?"

"I'm terribly sorry, my friends." Fridjof hung his head. "But I do have one consolation to offer. I know some of you are aware that I own the palace at the edge of town."

Moyra noticed that Fridjof avoided any mention of the ruins, even though the ice palace was located near there.

"Tonight," Fridjof boomed, "I will hold a great feast there. You are all invited to dine as my guests."

A cheer went up from the crowd. Fridjof waited for the noise to die down and continued, "There will be wondrous delicacies to eat. We will have dancing. And you will all be able to see my beautiful collection of snow globes."

"He's inviting everyone to a feast?" Moyra whispered. "He's always trying so hard to impress everyone with his wealth. What a jerk!"

Driskoll looked at Moyra skeptically. "I think it's nice."

"Yeah," Kellach said. "Why are you so critical of him? He saved Driskoll's life!"

Moyra hung her head, but she didn't answer. The boys would never understand.

The crowd dispersed, chatting happily about the feast ahead.

Moyra watched Fridjof carefully. He was whispering to his dwarf companion, and he looked at her once, his eyes gleaming cold.

"I wish Zendric were here," Moyra said. "He would know what to do." Moyra touched the amulet she wore around her neck. It made her feel safe to have it there, within reach if she needed it.

"So let's go find him," Kellach said, pulling on her arm.

"We need to solve the next riddle," Moyra said.

"What makes you so sure solving the riddle will help us find Zendric?" Driskoll asked. "We don't even know whether Zendric wanted us to have the amulets."

"Just a hunch," Moyra replied. "But it's all we have to go on. Read the clue again, Kellach."

Kellach pulled the cloth out and read aloud: "'Round and round, a shape without end, you will find this fire with a friend.'"

Kellach looked up. "Round and round, a shape without end? That's a ring!"

"A ring on the finger of a friend maybe? Whose friend? Zendric's friend?" Moyra asked.

"I didn't know Zendric had any friends," Driskoll said mischievously. "I know he has plenty of enemies."

"Of course, he has friends. He has plenty of friends. He has us," Kellach said.

"And your father," Moyra added. "But maybe it means our friends, or the friends of the Knights."

"We need to go back to the tower," Kellach said suddenly. "I think I know what Zendric means."

Once inside the tower, Kellach led them to a large statue of a warrior queen. The statue stood near the back of the workroom. There were golden hoops in her ears and a heavy golden band around one biceps.

"The statue is as tall as you are, Kellach," Driskoll said. "Who is she?"

"This is a statue of Boudica. She was a friend of Zendric's who fought bravely during the time of the Sundering of the Seal. She disappeared in the ruins a short time after. Whenever Zendric passes this statue, he bows and says 'good morning, my old friend'. Zendric does not have many old friends left." Kellach explained.

The children carefully searched the statue.

"There aren't any rings on her fingers," Moyra said. "Are you sure we are at the right place?"

"I'm sure," Kellach said. "I can't think of any other old friend."

"I'm beginning to think she's laughing at us," Moyra said, looking at the statue in exasperation. "Maybe we should go."

She wished they could leave the tower. What if Kellach or Driskoll found the diamond she'd hidden?

"What about the bookshelves?" Driskoll suggested. "Maybe the amulet is hidden in one of Zendric's favorite books?"

"No!" Moyra cried and stepped in front of Driskoll.

Driskoll looked at her, puzzled. "What's wrong with you, Moyra?"

"I . . . I just mean I'm sure it's in the statue. Let's keep looking here."

Kellach nodded, sitting down by Boudica's foot. "I know it's here somewhere. I can feel it. I feel like we're missing something."

"Like what?" Moyra asked.

"Like . . . ," Kellach said. He stopped speaking and stared up at the statue.

"What is it?" Driskoll and Moyra called out together.

"Rings." Kellach said and pointed to the statue's ears. "Earrings." He reached out and tugged on one of the earrings. The earring came off easily. Kellach held it up for them to see. A small black stone dangled from the hoop. They looked closely. The fire symbol was etched onto the rock.

"That's it!" Moyra said.

Kellach looked disappointed. "I don't have pierced ears. I can't wear it."

"I have pierced ears," Moyra said. "I'll trade you." Kellach and Moyra exchanged amulets.

"I like earrings better anyway," Moyra said.

"Was that all that was there?" Driskoll asked. "Usually there's another clue."

Moyra started to put on the earring amulet. "Wait a minute. There's a scrap inside the hoop!" she said. She took out a tiny piece of parchment.

"'If anything happens to me,'" Moyra read, "'find Thelonius.'"

"I knew that grumpy old man was suspicious!" Driskoll said.

"Zendric's practically telling us Thelonius kidnapped him."

Moyra looked at Kellach. "Now what?"

"Now we find Zendric," Kellach said.

CHAPTER

15

The Flying Dragon was full of visitors when they stepped in, but there was no sign of the scowling innkeeper.

"So what exactly are we looking for?" Driskoll whispered as they pushed through a crowd of elves decked out with expensive furs.

"I don't know," Kellach said. "Any indication that Zendric is here. I think Thelonius may be holding him captive here."

"Just keep quiet so Thelonius doesn't notice us," Moyra said as they entered the library alcove. "Whatever we're looking for, if he finds us first, we're—"

Moyra felt a tap on her shoulder. Slowly she turned.

There, standing before her was Thelonius.

"I thought I told you kids that I don't loan out my books," Thelonius said in a low voice. Then strangely, he smiled. "But I'm glad you're here."

Driskoll's eyes went wide. "Y-you are?"

Thelonius yanked him by the arm. "Yes, come with me," he said in a harsh voice. "I have something to show you." He guided the children along, moving past the library, nodding and smiling at the patrons as he went.

Soon, they were in the distant part of the inn, where it was quiet. There was no one else around. Their footsteps echoed down the hall.

"Where are you taking us?" Moyra asked. She chewed her fingers nervously, then she touched the small dagger she carried at all times.

"I mean you no harm, child," the innkeeper said.

The kids looked at one another doubtfully. The innkeeper probably wanted to throw them in some room and leave them to rot.

"I once did a service to the Knights of the Silver Dragon, and because of this, I earned their trust. I've been saving something for you."

Thelonius stopped in front of a small oak door and pulled out a set of keys. He inserted one of the keys into the lock, opened the door, and motioned for them to enter.

Moyra looked up at the innkeeper. He seemed pleasant enough, but why did he want them to enter this tiny room? Moyra peered in through the door. The walls were lined with bookshelves. The books looked older than those in the other part of the inn.

"Please, children, after you," Thelonius said.

Moyra's eyes narrowed, and she held up her fists. "We'll go with you, but you'll be sorry if you touch a hair on anyone's head."

The innkeeper said quietly, "Your loyalty does you credit, but I do not have any evil intentions. I'm sorry if I yelled at you earlier. I simply never expected Zendric to send children. Now, please." Thelonius motioned them toward the room.

The three kids looked at one other warily and crossed the threshold into the tiny library.

"Do you know where Zendric went?" Driskoll asked, but the innkeeper did not reply for a moment.

"Everyone has secrets," the innkeeper said gently. Moyra thought he was referring to her when he said it. "I've simply been keeping one secret until the Knights were ready to claim it again."

Moyra shivered at the mention of secrets. The innkeeper's violet eyes grew solemn. He stared into her eyes until she thought he could see her soul.

"What is this place?" she asked.

"Ah," Thelonius puffed out his chest and gestured to the bookshelves, "these books are the oldest and rarest books in Curston. After the Sundering of the Seal, everything belonging to the Knights was scattered."

Kellach nudged Moyra. She knew what he was thinking. They might be able to find more clues about Zendric's disappearance.

"Zendric was . . . occupied elsewhere at the time, so I began collecting objects that I thought had once belonged to the Knights. Eventually, I was able to purchase the items you see here," he said.

"What did you want to show us?" she asked. She felt

trapped in the tiny room and trapped by the weight of all the secrets.

"First I must ask something of you." Thelonius poked his head out the door and scanned the corridor. Satisfied, he whispered, "Have you found them?"

"Found what?" Moyra asked.

The old innkeeper leaned in closer. Moyra could smell his stinky breath. "The amulets, child. Where are they? I need them."

Kellach, Moyra, and Driskoll exchanged glances.

"Uh, we . . ." Driskoll began reaching into his pocket, but Moyra poked him in the ribs.

"We don't have them," Moyra said, giving Driskoll and Kellach a pointed glare.

Thelonius sighed. "I thought so." He hung his head and muttered, "Why Zendric chose children, I'll never understand."

He straightened up and took a thick book off the shelf. "I suppose it won't do any harm to give you this. At least you'll learn something." Thelonius looked down at them skeptically. "You are the Knights of the Silver Dragon, correct?"

Kellach stood a little straighter. "Of course we are."

Thelonius nodded. "Then this is for you. Guard it well," he said.

Moyra's head snapped up at the words. That was the same thing Zendric had said to Kellach at the market the last time they saw him. Was it just a coincidence that Thelonius used those words?

He placed the book in Kellach's hands. The book was filthy

with dust. It looked like it hadn't been opened since before the Sundering of the Seal.

Bowing politely, Thelonius excused himself and left them in the room.

Kellach swept the dust off the cover of the ancient book. "The Story of the Knights of the Silver Dragon," he said, reading the title. "Wow! I wonder if we're in here." He began to open the book, but Moyra laid her hand over it, slamming it shut.

"Quick, let's get out of here."

Kellach looked shocked. "But what about the book?"

"We can read that later." She poked her head out into the hallway. Driskoll and Kellach crowded into the doorway with her.

Moyra watched the innkeeper walk down the hallway.

"Let's follow him," she said.

"What?" Driskoll said. "Why?"

"Because I don't trust that man," Moyra said. "How did he know about our amulets? And what was all that about secrets? I think Thelonius knows something he's not telling us."

CHAPTER

16

As soon as the innkeeper turned the corner at the end of the hallway, Moyra motioned with her hand for Driskoll and Kellach to follow her. Thelonius went up the stairs and down a long corridor. The three kids tiptoed several paces behind him. He never looked back.

Eventually he turned a corner ahead of them. Kellach, Moyra, and Driskoll crept forward cautiously. Together they peered around the corner into the adjoining hall.

But the corridor was completely empty. The innkeeper was gone.

"Where did he go?" Driskoll asked, pacing up and down the hall.

"Keep your voice down," Kellach warned in a low voice.

"But it doesn't make any sense!" Driskoll said, this time speaking in a low whisper. "There's only one door here." He motioned toward the end of the corridor, where a set of double doors stood wide open. "But I can see from here there's no one in there!"

"Maybe there's a hidden door," Moyra said.

She put her ear to the wall. Suddenly, she looked back at the boys, her eyes wide.

"I can hear voices," she whispered.

Moyra put her ear back to the wall. "It's Thelonius. And there's someone else in the room with him. But I can't tell what they're saying."

She gasped. "Wait! I just heard Zendric's name!"

Kellach stuck his ear to the wall, and his brother copied him.

"I can't hear anything," Driskoll complained.

Abruptly, the voices stopped.

"Hide!" Moyra said. "They've stopped talking." She grabbed Driskoll by the collar and ran for the double doors at the end of the corridor, with Kellach right behind them.

They found themselves in an elaborate bedroom. Moyra walked over to the poster bed and sat on its goose down cover.

"This must be one of the inn's best rooms," Driskoll said. "I wonder who has stayed here? A king or a famous warrior?"

"Who cares?" Moyra said. "We'd better concentrate on getting out of here without getting caught."

They heard the soft sound of a door sliding open and closed. Moyra slowly peered out into the hallway. The innkeeper was rounding the corner out of sight.

"He's gone," she said. "He was alone, though. I swore I heard him talking to someone. The other voice sounded male. Almost like Zendric's voice."

"Maybe it *was* Zendric!" Driskoll said. "Kellach was right.

Thelonius is keeping Zendric captive! We've got to help him."

"There must be another door somewhere," Kellach said thoughtfully. "Let's try to find it."

After making sure the coast was clear. Moyra went down the hall and ran her fingers along the wall. Driskoll and Kellach followed behind her.

After a few minutes of searching, Moyra sat down in the center of the corridor. "This is hopeless. We're never going to find it."

She stared blankly ahead of her. A tall tapestry hung from the ceiling, covering the wall in front of her all the way to the floor. It depicted a silver dragon flying over what looked like an ancient map of Curston.

Driskoll sidled up next to her. "That's a strange spot for a tapestry. Normally, they hang those things in dining halls."

Moyra took in a quick breath. "Wait a minute! I've got it!"

She ran across the hall and tugged at the edge of the thick cloth. It wouldn't budge.

"Help me pull the tapestry back," she called to Kellach and Driskoll. "This thing weighs a ton."

Kellach and Driskoll each took a corner and lifted the heavy woven cloth as high as they could.

Moyra gasped. "This is it! We found it!"

There, in the wall, was a small oak door. At the center was a carving of a dragon. In its claw, the dragon held a silver orb, similar to a small doorknob.

"Zendric, we're coming!" Moyra pressed down on the orb and heard a click as a door slid open.

CHAPTER

17

Moyra ducked through the door and stepped into a narrow little room, with Kellach and Driskoll right behind her.

Bookshelves lined the wall. A miniature astronomical clock sat atop a small table, which was scattered with old books. More books were scattered all over the floor. In the corner of the room, sat a narrow cot. A blanket lay tangled at the bottom of the straw mattress as if someone had recently rolled out of bed.

"There's no one here!" Moyra said. "But where could he have gone?"

Driskoll walked over to the cot and kicked it. "Obviously, someone is—was hiding here."

There was a large vase stuffed full of faded scrolls in a corner. Kellach immediately wandered over to them and began to read.

Moyra studied some of the objects on the shelves. She came face to face with a grinning dragon skull and recoiled.

"What is this?" Driskoll asked. Moyra glanced over at Driskoll. He seemed strangely distracted and was staring at a faint mark of a dragon painted near the bottom of one wall.

"It's nothing," Moyra said. "C'mon, let's go."

"Yes, it is. It's a mark," Driskoll persisted. Moyra looked to where he pointed. When she moved closer, she saw the faint tracing of a silver dragon painted on the woodwork.

"There's a mark just like this one in a room in Zendric's tower and in the library here at the Flying Dragon," Driskoll said.

"So?" Moyra said.

"Didn't you notice how nervous Thelonius got when I touched it?" Driskoll said. "I think there's another way out of this room. He's hiding something, that's for sure."

They grinned at each other. "We're close, I can feel it!" Driskoll said.

They tapped the wall in a variety of places, but nothing happened. Moyra and Driskoll finally sat down on the cot, discouraged.

"I give up," Driskoll said. "We've looked all over, but nothing budged. If there's another hidden door, it's concealed very well."

"Let's get out of here," Moyra said. "We'll try again later."

They walked out of the room, heads down. As they left, Moyra thought she caught a glimpse of Thelonius's black curls rounding the corner.

■ ▪ ▮ ▪ ▮

It was still early when the children exited the Flying Dragon and headed down Visitor Street. The morning sun, which had been missing almost as long as Zendric, sent down feeble rays of sunshine.

Moyra looked up at Kellach. "So what do we do now?"

Kellach pulled his scarf tighter around his neck. "Let's get out of this freezing cold and investigate that book Thelonius gave us. Maybe there's a clue in there."

Driskoll walked a few paces behind them, staring at the cobblestone road. "I'm sure I remember seeing that symbol in Zendric's tower. Somewhere."

As they rounded the corner, Moyra let out a little cry. "Look there's your dad!" She nudged Kellach and pointed to two men coming down the road toward them. Torin was engaged in conversation with Kalmbur, another watcher. Neither of them looked up.

"Quick, duck behind those barrels," Kellach said.

The two men walked closer. As they neared the barrels, Kalmbur slowed to light his pipe. Torin kept on talking, and Moyra could hear every word of the conversation.

"I saw the evidence with my own eyes, but I don't want to believe it," Torin said.

"Where was it found?" said Kalmbur, as his blew out his match.

"The pin was in one of the missing supply wagons. They were looted and abandoned about two miles out on the southern road. No trace of the driver," Torin said.

Kalmbur puffed on his pipe. "Does anyone else have a Knight

of the Silver Dragon pin?"

"Just my children and Moyra. I checked, and they all still have theirs. It's Zendric's all right."

"It looks bad for Zendric," Kalmbur said.

Torin nodded. "That old business with the theft of the diamond won't help Zendric's case. People in Curston have a long memory."

Moyra bit her lip to keep from gasping at the mention of the diamond.

Kalmbur looked surprised. "What diamond?"

Torin answered, "It was before my time, but some people still remember that Zendric was accused of stealing a large blue diamond from the Knights of the Silver Dragon. As far as I understand, they never found any evidence against him, and Zendric was cleared."

Moyra's stomach twisted. Zendric had been accused of stealing a diamond? Was it the same diamond as the one she had found? It had to be, and yet she couldn't believe Zendric would ever steal anything, especially not from the Knights of the Silver Dragon.

"Zendric's the only Knight left now, though," Kalmbur said, "isn't he? There's no one else who would have a Knights pin."

"It's worrisome to say the least." Torin rubbed his chin. "Let's keep this quiet as long as possible. We need to give Zendric a chance to return to clear his name."

The two men resumed walking down the street, turned the corner, and slipped out of sight.

The three Knights slid out of their hiding place.

Moyra looked at the two boys. She knew then she couldn't keep her secret any longer. She needed to tell them about the diamond. It couldn't wait another day. Zendric's life might depend on it.

"Kellach, Driskoll," she said solemnly. "Follow me. I think I need to show you something."

CHAPTER

18

They arrived at Zendric's tower in record time, spurred by the freezing wind. Moyra sidled up to the bookcase. She stared at the books, trying to figure out where to begin her story.

The boys exchanged glances.

"Moyra, why don't you just tell us what's been bothering you," Kellach said.

"Yeah," Driskoll added, "you've been acting weird."

Moyra stuck out her tongue at Driskoll, and they all laughed. The shared laughter eased the tension in Moyra, and she took a deep breath. They were her friends. They would understand. It was hurting her too much to keep a secret for so long.

She turned to face Kellach. "Do you remember the day Zendric let you out early? The day we had the snowball fight?"

"Of course," Kellach replied, "that was the last time we saw Zendric."

"Remember, you threw that big snowball at me? Well, when I looked down on the ground, I found another snowball. But it was hard. And heavy. At first, I just thought it was a big rock."

The boys nodded. If Moyra weren't so nervous, she would have giggled at the sight of Driskoll and Kellach nodding in time.

"But when I wiped off the snow, I realized it wasn't a rock. It was a diamond. A blue diamond as big as my fist." She doubled up her fist to demonstrate.

"A diamond?" Driskoll exclaimed. "But that's great. You can sell it and help your family!"

"That's what I thought. But I was afraid it was cursed. I was going to ask Zendric about it before I tried to sell it. But then he disappeared. And the cold snap continued. And . . ." Moyra hung her head and tried to hold back the tears. "This is all my fault."

"Moyra," Kellach put a hand on her shoulder. "Slow down. You're not making any sense."

Moyra nodded and wiped her eyes.

Kellach lifted her chin and looked her directly in the eyes. "Where's the diamond now?"

"I hid it," Moyra explained. "I was scared my mom would find it and sell it. She's been acting so weird lately. All lovey-dovey with that creep Fridjof."

Driskoll jumped back. "What do you mean? Fridjof's no creep. He saved my life!"

Kellach ignored him. "Where did you hide the diamond, Moyra?"

"It's right here." She turned and faced the bookcase. "I decided Zendric's tower was safer." She grabbed a book, pulled it out, and reached for her coin purse.

Moyra opened the pouch and took out the diamond. It gleamed blue in the sunlight.

"That diamond is enormous," Driskoll said. "That would fetch a fortune in the open market."

"And it's blue," Kellach said. "Dad said Zendric was accused of stealing a blue diamond. Moyra, what if your diamond is the same one?"

Moyra nodded sullenly. "That's what I wondered, too."

"But how will we ever know?" Driskoll asked. "The only one who would know is Zendric and he's . . ." But Driskoll couldn't bear to finish the thought.

Moyra brightened. "The book! The one Thelonius gave us. It was called *The Story of the Knights of the Silver Dragon*. Maybe there's something about it in there!"

"Good idea!" Kellach settled into one of Zendric's armchairs. He opened the book releasing a large puff of dust. "Now let's see. There's a lot of information here." He leafed through the pages, skimming the text at record speed. At last he gave a little cry.

"Aha!" he said. "Listen to this." And he began to read:

One of the darkest episodes in our order's history came when our dear Zendric was accused of stealing the Diamond of Destruction. An uncut blue diamond the size of a child's fist, the gem has the power to wield devastation over entire cities. Unearthed from the bowels of the legendary Shadow Caves by an evil wizard, the gemstone had been confiscated by the Knights of the Silver Dragon and held in their protection for centuries. Then one day, the diamond disappeared. Only one Knight, Zendric, had the key to unlock the secret safehold where the diamond was kept. He was accused of the crime, but no one could ever prove he did it. To this day, the crime remains unsolved.

Kellach looked up. "Gods! Moyra, if that diamond is what I think it is, this is really serious."

Moyra's eyes widened as she stared at the diamond in her hand. "Do you think it's really the Diamond of Destruction?"

"Only one way to find out," Kellach said. "We need to test it."

Kellach grabbed for the gem, but Moyra pulled her hand back instinctively. "Are you insane? If you set this thing off, it might destroy all of Curston!"

Kellach laughed. "Relax. I just need to see if there's a magic aura around it." He cracked his knuckles. "Trust me. It's harmless. Even Driskoll could do this spell."

Driskoll gave his brother a shove. "Very funny."

"If you say so." Moyra handed the diamond to her friend.

Kellach closed his eyes and began to whisper under his breath.

An instant later, a white cone of light sprouted from the diamond. The cone grew wider and taller and into a twirling, swirling wind. The wind picked up off the diamond, turning into a loud howl that hurt their ears.

The floor shook, and the doors and windows banged. Books flew off the bookshelves. The wind tilted and turned into a funnel cloud, moving this way and that almost as if trying to escape the room. The heavy furniture scraped across the floor and slammed against the walls.

"Hold on to something heavy," Moyra screamed above the roar.

She ducked as a chair flew by, narrowly missing her head. Driskoll and Moyra clung to Zendric's worktable, which was made of mahogany and weighed about a ton. Driskoll's legs dangled in the wind as he held on tightly to avoid joining the objects dancing crazily in the air.

"Turn it off!" Driskoll yelled at his brother.

Kellach's eyes were wide as he gripped the edge of the bookcase. "I'm not sure how! I've never done this spell on something this powerful before!"

Kellach desperately grabbed a book out of the air and held it down, turning the pages. "I'll look for something," he shouted above the noise. "Anything to make it STOP!"

All at once, all motion ceased. The roaring dervish disappeared.

The books landed with a thud on the carpet, narrowly missing Moyra's head. A statue dropped right into Driskoll's hands. The only sound in the room was the sound of their own breathing.

Moyra looked around the room. Although it looked like a giant child had flung everything down in a fit, nothing was broken.

She put her hands on her hips and gave Kellach a long stare. "A simple spell, eh?"

"What did you say?" Driskoll said in a loud voice. He put a finger in his ear. There was a popping noise. "That's better. I can hear again."

Kellach cleared his throat. "I admit I underestimated how powerful the aura would be. But this is most definitely the Diamond of Destruction. And judging by the power of the aura,"—he held the blue diamond up to the light—"this jewel could not only lay waste to Curston but to every city and town within a hundred leagues."

Just then, they heard shouts and the sounds of stomping boots outside the window.

Driskoll ran to the windowsill and leaned out.

"Uh-oh. We've got trouble. It's Dad."

CHAPTER

19

Moyra and Kellach ran to the window to get a better look. Torin, along with a troupe of watchers, was marching down the street.

"Surround the tower!" Torin barked, pointing up at Zendric's home. "And for Cuthbert's sake, Kalmbur, call in the reinforcements!"

Moyra whipped her head around and stared at Kellach. "He must have noticed all the commotion caused by that spell!"

Driskoll's eyes went wide. "If Dad catches us in here, he'll be livid. He'll have us clean the latrines for the rest of our natural lives!"

"We'll have to delay them," Kellach said. "I'll create a diversion. Then we'll sneak out."

"What are you going to do?" Moyra said.

Kellach smiled. "I have an idea. You two stand back and wait until I give the word."

Moyra stomped her foot. "Not on your life. I'm not moving

one inch from this window, in case you don't get the spell right."
Moyra scowled. "Again."

"Have it your way." Kellach whispered something under his breath and traced the gesture of a spell in the air.

Instantly, the sky lit with sparks of red, green, and even purple. The sparks danced into magical shapes: first a dragon, then a unicorn.

Torin took one look up at the sky, and then he glanced back at his men. "There's a magic user laying siege on Zendric's tower. Move! Surround the tower!"

But the watchers were transfixed by the sparkling sky.

"Now," Kellach whispered. "Quickly, while they're distracted."

Moyra began to rush for the door, then she stopped. Something was wrong. "Kellach! Where's Driskoll?"

Kellach's head whipped around the room. "He's gone!"

"Driskoll, where are you?" Moyra called. "This is no time for hide and seek."

With a click, a door sprang out of the fieldstone fireplace, and Driskoll appeared. "Look! A hidden passageway," he explained. He stepped into the room and touched something in the door, and it sprang back into the mantelpiece, revealing the symbol of a silver dragon on the stonework.

"It's just like the symbol at the Flying Dragon," Kellach said.

"And I'd bet my last gold coin that if we follow the passage, it will lead there," Driskoll added.

They stared at the door for a moment.

"Well, what are we waiting for?" Moyra shrugged. "If nothing else, it's the perfect escape route."

She pressed her hand on the impression of the silver dragon. The door clicked open, and the three children stepped into darkness.

CHAPTER

20

Kellach led the way, holding an ever-burning torch he'd borrowed from Zendric's tower. The narrow passageway was barely wide enough for the three of them to walk abreast. The flame from the torch cast just enough light for them to take in their surroundings.

The walls and floor were of smooth stone and covered in moss in places. Huge cobwebs hung above them, and there was dust everywhere.

"This place is filthy," Moyra said. She sneezed loudly.

As they walked along the corridor, the path sloped downward sharply. The air grew colder and damper. After several minutes of steady walking, the path finally evened out.

"It feels like we've been walking for miles," Moyra said.

"I think we're underneath the city now," Kellach said.

"It doesn't look like anybody has even been here in ages," Driskoll said.

"Oh, yes it does," Kellach said. He pointed to the ground,

where a set of footprints was outlined in the dust. He stooped and ran his fingers over the ground.

"It looks like these were made by a wizard's slippers." Kellach looked up.

"Zendric's?" Driskoll asked.

Kellach shrugged. "There's no way of knowing for sure. It could be Zendric's. Or it could be some other wizard's."

"An evil wizard?" Moyra shivered.

"We should be very quiet," Kellach said. "Whoever left these could still be here."

They crept along the dark corridor. The air grew even colder. They followed the prints along the path.

Something shiny caught Moyra's eye. She bent down and picked it up.

Moyra stared at the object in her hand. "It's a Knight of the Silver Dragon pin!"

She held it out for the boys to see.

"It looks like Zendric's," Kellach said.

"Hang on," Driskoll said. "Didn't Dad say a Silver Dragon pin was found in the missing supply wagons? How could there be two pins?"

"Maybe there's another Knight somewhere?" Moyra looked concerned. "Maybe whoever sabotaged those wagons was a Knight. But not like us. A Knight who turned evil."

Driskoll's eyes widened. "Could it be Thelonius? It makes sense. I mean how does he have all that Knights of the Silver Dragon information?"

Kellach punched him in the shoulder. "Don't be ridiculous,

you two. If there were any others Knights around, we would know about it."

Moyra flipped the pin over. On the back, something had been engraved on the surface, The silver was tarnished black, but she could make out the letter *Z*.

She looked up. "I don't know whose pin that was in the supply wagon, but this one's definitely Zendric's."

Driskoll gasped. "Zendric would never let someone take his Knight of the Silver Dragon's pin," he said. "He'd fight with the last breath in his body."

"That's what I'm afraid of," Kellach said grimly. "Come on, we're on the right track. Let's keep going."

They walked for a few more paces in silence, with Kellach leading the way. Moyra gripped the dragon pin in her hand, thinking about poor Zendric. Why would he have used these tunnels? What was he running away from? And where was he headed?

Moyra was so lost in her thoughts that she didn't notice when Kellach came to a stop in front of her.

"Watch it!" Kellach said as she bumped into his back.

"Sorry," she said sheepishly. She looked up to see what the delay was.

Here, the path dissected into three new corridors. Each corridor had the silver dragon symbol carved into the stone above the arch.

"Which way?" Moyra asked.

"I'm not sure." Kellach squatted down and cast the light from the torch onto the ground in front of him. "The footprints are obscured here. I can't tell which way he went."

Driskoll looked up at the arches. "Look at those dragons up there. I think these tunnels belong to the Knights."

Kellach brushed the dust off his robes and stood up. "It makes sense."

"And if I'm right," Driskoll said, "one of these passages leads to the inn. The Flying Dragon would be the perfect escape route when Zendric or any other Knight needed to leave Curston in secret. You could disguise yourself as an out-of-town visitor, borrow a horse from the inn's stables, and be off before anyone was the wiser."

"Maybe that's what Zendric did," Kellach said. "Nobody saw him leave, at least as far as I've been able to find out."

Moyra peered down the far left corridor, then the one straight in front of her. "So which one of these passages do you think leads to the Flying Dragon?" Moyra asked. "Maybe this one?" She took a few steps down the corridor to the right.

"Phew, what is that smell?" Kellach asked.

"I smell it too." Moyra sniffed loudly. "It's like rotten onions and dirt."

"Sh! I hear something," Kellach said.

"What? I don't hear anything!" Driskoll said as the ground began to shake.

In the distance, a low rumble echoed off the walls. Bits of rock and dirt shook loose from the ceiling of the tunnel and rained down on their heads. A strange white light appeared, casting a sickly haze upon the three kids' faces.

"Look over there!" Moyra said, pointing down the right-hand corridor.

Heading their way, its skin glowing an eerie white, was an enormous worm. As it slithered through the underground passage, the tunnel's foundations began to shift. With each contraction of its body, another beam support cracked.

"I don't believe it!" Kellach cried. "What would a frost worm be doing down here?"

"What can we do to fight a frost worm?" Moyra yelled over the growing rumble.

"Run!" Kellach shouted. "If that thing catches up to us, it will swallow us whole!"

Moyra turned to look down the right-hand corridor. It was a mistake. Moving with incredible speed, the worm was almost upon them.

"Which way?" Driskoll said.

"It doesn't matter. We need to get out of here now!" Moyra yanked hard on Driskoll's arm, flinging him down the far left corridor.

Moyra heard something clatter to the ground. The pin! It had fallen out of her hand when she grabbed Driskoll.

She fell to her knees and frantically ran her palms over the freezing stone floor. "Wait! I dropped Zendric's pin!" If only it weren't so dark. She felt as if she were blind.

"Moyra!" Kellach called back. "Just leave it! We've got to go now!"

The worm's sickly light cast a glow across the floor.

Hah, Moyra thought. She could almost see clearly now.

"Give me one more second!" She ran her fingers along one edge of the passageway, where the wall met the ground. Nothing.

As the worm oozed its way closer, the smell of dead leaves, old garbage, and moist dirt almost made her gag.

She knew it was now or never. She pressed her back against the wall and pushed herself up to stand. As she did, she felt something catch against the back of her pants.

She leaned forward to run. But her right leg held fast against the cold stone wall.

"Moyra!" Driskoll screamed. "The worm!"

"I'm stuck," Moyra said, tugging desperately at her leg. "My pants! I think somehow the fabric wedged between the stones in the wall."

The worm was so close that Moyra could see its great gaping red mouth.

"Your amulet!" Kellach cried. "Use the amulet!"

Moyra's hand flew to the leather cord around her neck.

But it wasn't there.

Her chest tightened, and she felt like she could barely breathe. After everything they'd been through, she was going to die here—a slimy, frost worm's last meal.

The worm stopped in front of her and lifted its head as if sniffing her scent. Moyra tugged desperately at her pant leg. Come on. Come on. She felt her heart pounding in her ears.

Her ears! In a flash she remembered she had traded her amulet necklace with Kellach. Her fingers scrambled to grasp the earring piercing her ear. She tugged on her ear lobe, pointing the tiny black stone at the vile creature's slimy mouth.

"Emalf!" she screamed. "Emalf!"

Instantly, a bright flame erupted from the miniature amulet and flew through the air, searing the frost worm's skin. The worm recoiled.

Moyra didn't hesitate. With one last resounding rip, she pulled her pant leg free and barreled down the corridor after her two friends.

Together, the three Knights ran as if their very lives depended upon it. They all knew that, although wounded, the frost worm wouldn't be deterred for long.

In the distance, Moyra could hear the frost worm's high-pitched scream. Seconds later, the deep rumble began again.

"It's coming after us!" Moyra shouted at Kellach.

"Here!" Kellach pulled her around the corner into an adjoining corridor. They pressed themselves against the wall.

As they heard the large worm approach, Moyra stiffened. What if it saw them?

Kellach seemed to read her mind. "It's okay," he whispered. "I think it's actually a baby frost worm. The adults are far bigger, if you can believe it. The babies don't have very good vision. Just don't move, and it won't know we're here. "

They huddled in the corridor and watched the frost worm pass in front of their hiding spot. They heard the sound of cracking beams and falling rocks.

After a few moments, Kellach dared to lean out into the passageway. "It's gone."

Moyra drew a shaky breath. "That was a close one."

"Yes, it was," Kellach said as they walked down the corridor in which they had been hiding. "It seems we have more questions than before. What was a frost worm doing in these tunnels? Its natural habitat lies far to the north."

"Someone must have deliberately sent the worm down here," Driskoll said.

"No one knew we were here," Moyra said.

"Is that true?" Kellach said. "What about Thelonius? He knew we were at the inn and looking for clues about Zendric's disappearance."

"I didn't say anything because I didn't think it mattered," Moyra admitted, "but I'm pretty sure I saw Thelonius when we came out of the hidden room the other day. I think he was spying on us. He could have overheard us."

"But where would an innkeeper get a frost worm?" Driskoll asked.

"You're right," Kellach said thoughtfully. "It would take a wizard to call a frost worm and bring it under control."

"A wizard? You don't suspect Zendric, do you?" Driskoll asked.

"Of course not." Kellach scoffed. "But we're dealing with someone who has magical powers. And this person is not feeling very friendly toward us right now, whoever he or she is."

Moyra sighed. "We can figure all that out later. What matters now is how are we going to get out of here? This place is a maze."

Driskoll patted her back. "Don't worry, Moyra. I've got it covered. I'm almost positive now these are secret Knights' tunnels. They all lead somewhere."

Moyra looked at him skeptically.

"You'll see," he said.

The three kids walked along in silence for a few minutes until at last they came to a small door. As expected, a small silver dragon was stamped on the front.

"I told you!" Driskoll said. He opened the door cautiously. "Just what I thought," he crowed. "We're back at the room in the inn."

They crouched through the doorway. The cot was now made up neatly, and the books were all gone.

"Thelonius must know we found the hidden room after all," Driskoll said.

"Or someone." Kellach absently walked over to the table and rubbed his finger along the astronomical clock on the table.

Suddenly, he snapped to attention. "Gods! It's almost time for Fridjof's feast. We had better get going. Dad will be furious if we miss it."

"We can't miss it!" Driskoll ran for the door. "I heard there will be roast pig and mashed potatoes, and a seven-layer cake." He looked back at Moyra. "If we head for Main Square right now, we could be on the first wagon train."

The rough cloth flapped against Moyra's skin where her pant had ripped. She remembered the dress Fridjof had given her, and her heart skipped a beat. At last, she'd have a good excuse to wear it.

She looked at Driskoll. "Are you kidding? I can't go like this!" She turned and displayed her ripped pant. "My pants are ruined. I have to change and meet you there."

Driskoll looked at her as if she'd lost her mind. "What do you mean? Since when do you care what you look like?"

Moyra wondered too. But that lovely dress called to her, begging to be worn.

CHAPTER

21

An hour later, Moyra stood in front of the frozen fountain in the entryway of Fridjof's ice palace. She smoothed the skirt of her new dress nervously. It almost felt like she was petting a cloud. The rich purple velvet was the softest material she'd ever touched. And it was warm! Thanks to the dress, she hadn't needed to wear her father's heavy coat, although she had grabbed the bilious green scarf and reluctantly wrapped it around her bare neck. It was a shame to ruin the look of the dress with such an ugly scarf. But it was all she had.

She lifted her long skirt up a few inches and took another look at the elegant slippers she wore. She wiggled her toes and the soft leather shimmered. She almost didn't recognize her own feet. She couldn't remember the last time she'd felt so . . . pretty.

She wrapped her green scarf a bit tighter around her neck and adjusted the clip in her hair one more time.

Now, where were those boys? She peered around the icy fountain.

The palace was filled to the brim with people. The long banquet table they'd seen the first time they were there had been moved to the front of the room. It stood now on a small platform, looking down on what seemed to be dozens of round tables dotting the giant room. The tables were set in a circular pattern. At the front of the room, near the host's table, a space had been left empty for a dance floor.

It looked like every soul in Curston was already seated at the round ice tables. The chairs were draped with silver furs, and there were vases of lilies on every table. Huge tapestries of hunting wolves hung from the ceiling. Moyra could smell roast pig. Her stomach growled in response.

She marched toward one of the tables. She swung her arms, and her sleeves swished softly. The dress seemed to whisper as she walked.

"Moyra!" Driskoll and Kellach came running up to greet her.

"We've been waiting for ever!" Driskoll said. "What took you so long?" Suddenly, Driskoll stopped and looked Moyra up and down. "Wow, you look . . . different."

"Different?" she said.

"Where'd you get that outfit?" Kellach asked. "I've never seen you look so . . . feminine."

"Oh this old thing?" Moyra lifted the skirt and patted her hair. "I . . . I know it's much too girly for me, but it's all I had to wear after my pants were torn."

"Well, you look great," Kellach said gruffly. "You're the best-dressed girl here."

She looked down so Kellach couldn't see her smile and quickly changed the subject.

"Come on," Moyra said. "Let's go sit down. By the time I got home, my mom had already left for the feast. But she left a note saying she'd save us seats."

Together, they pushed through the narrow space between the round tables.

"I can't believe it!" Moyra said. "Everyone is here."

"Everyone except Zendric," said Kellach sadly.

Torin saw them and gave them a brief wave before turning his attention to his duties, which was at the moment to stop Grellen from lunging for the roast pig.

"Wait for our host," Torin said sternly. The half-orc sat back down in his seat, chastened. Torin hurried off to deal with a more pressing problem—a small fight that had broken out between a young elf and her overly eager suitor.

Moyra scanned the crowd, searching for her mother. She waved to her godfather Patch who was holding a chair out for a pretty gnome dressed in a fur-lined gown. She saw Thelonius skulking by the stairwell.

"We'd better keep an eye on him," she whispered to Kellach. "If he really did kidnap Zendric, he might be after the diamond."

Kellach nodded. "It's possible. Where is the diamond? You left it at home, right?"

Moyra shook her head, but she didn't meet Kellach's eyes.

"You brought the diamond with you?" Kellach said. "Moyra? Are you cracked! It's crazy to carry that thing around with you."

"I . . . I didn't think it was safe to leave it." She couldn't tell him about the dress whispering to her to bring the jewel to the feast. He'd think she was crazy.

Luckily, at that moment, she spotted her mother waving them over to the table.

"Look there's my mom. Let's go."

"I've been holding these chairs forever. What took you so long?" Royma scolded. Her voice trailed off as she saw what her daughter wore. For a long moment, Royma just stared at her daughter. Moyra saw that tears had formed in her mother's eyes.

"Moyra, you look beautiful," Royma said. "Like a fairy princess."

"Thanks, Mom." Moyra slid into her chair, and Kellach and Driskoll took the two seats beside her. She smiled. "You do too."

Royma was wearing a red velvet dress, nearly as elegant as Moyra's. Moyra didn't have to ask where her mother had gotten such an expensive gown. She knew. Fridjof.

As if on cue, Fridjof appeared. He wore an elaborately embroidered tunic, gray with silver thread. There were jewels on every finger.

He bowed over Royma's hand. "My darling Royma, I'm so pleased that you could make it. You and your daughter." He flashed a smile in Moyra's direction. "You both look wonderful this evening."

Moyra felt guilt wash over her. She should never have accepted the dress. She should never have worn it. Now he thought she was her friend. She scowled.

But Fridjof didn't seem to notice. He looked deep into Royma's eyes. "There will be dancing after dinner. Would you honor me with a dance later this evening?"

Royma nodded and blushed, her questions forgotten. Moyra made a face when she thought her mother wasn't looking.

"Wonderful." Fridjof straightened. "Now I must be off. The duties of a host never end. He spread his arms wide. "I hope all of you will enjoy the meal!" And then he walked away.

Driskoll reached for a basket of bread, but Kellach smacked his hand. "You heard Dad. Wait until our host is seated. Really, Driskoll, your manners are about as good as that half-orc's."

"Well, yours are as good as—," Driskoll began, but the sound of a drum beating cut him short.

The crowd silenced, and everyone turned to the front of the room. Fridjof stood before the long table on the platform and began to speak.

"Welcome to my new home," Fridjof said. "You may not remember, but I lived in Curston as a boy. This feast is to thank you for all you did to, er, for me then."

The crowd clapped loudly at Fridjof's speech.

"That sounds odd," Moyra said.

What does?" Kellach replied.

"If Fridjof lived in Curston as a child, why doesn't anyone remember him?"

"Now," Fridjof continued, "I hope you will enjoy your meal. Please! Begin!" With that, he sat down.

A collective sigh of appreciation was heard as a dozen servants appeared, carrying silver platters filled with all sorts of delicacies. There were roast pigs with apples in their mouths, and platters piled with hot corn, mashed potatoes, roast chickens, and crispy sausages. Even Kellach's eyes grew round when a large baked peacock, complete with iridescent tail feathers, was set down on the table.

Driskoll began eagerly shoveling mashed potatoes onto his plate. He passed the bowl around the table.

Moyra ate slowly. She wasn't used to such rich food, and she didn't want to make herself sick, something it looked like Driskoll was well on his way to doing.

It seemed like every time one of their platters emptied, a servant arrived delivering more food.

"Fridjof must be wealthy indeed to be able to afford such a feast," Royma said, "I've never seen food like this before. It will be the talk of Curston for years to come."

A servant returned and filled their goblets with a rich drink that smelled like apple and honey.

Moyra held up a goblet and ran a thumb over the surface. "It's solid silver," she said.

A few minutes later, two servants placed a serving dish on their table. On it was a strange looking beast, with the body of a turkey and the head of a pig.

"What is that?" Moyra said.

"Do you think it's safe to eat?" Driskoll said.

Kellach shrugged. "I can't sense any magic. I suppose it's safe enough."

The words were barely out of Kellach's mouth before Driskoll had a plate piled high.

As his brother brought the first bite to his lips, Kellach said, "It could be poisoned, I guess."

Driskoll spewed food everywhere. Most of it landed on Kellach's face.

"And no more than you deserve," Royma said, wiping Kellach's face with the end of the tablecloth, "with that kind of talk. That's a gobbleswine. Gobbleswine isn't a magical beast. The cook sews half a turkey and half a pig together and then bakes it." Royma laughed.

Moyra thought her mother looked pretty when she laughed. The uncustomary smile wiped away Royma's perpetually worried look.

But as soon as the thought passed through her head, Royma's smile vanished. "What were you thinking teasing Driskoll like that?"

Kellach hung his head. He opened his mouth to speak, but at that moment, the orchestra of windup toy musicians started playing a waltz. They were the same musicians they had seen the day Fridjof arrived in town: the dog playing a flute, the donkey playing a drum, and the cat playing a guitar.

Royma clapped her hands in time to the music. "For a toy orchestra, this music is wonderful!"

"Whoever heard of a dog that plays the flute!" Moyra grumbled. She tried to enjoy the music, but she thought she heard a soft whispering.

"Did you hear that?" she asked Driskoll, who was eyeing the gingerbread dragons the servants had placed a few tables away.

He nodded. "Do you mean the sound of my stomach telling me it's time for dessert?" He chuckled happily as the servants returned with another tray full of cookies.

Fridjof materialized beside their table. "Are you enjoying yourselves?" he inquired politely.

"It's fantastic!" Driskoll exclaimed, his mouth half full with cookie.

Fridjof smiled and turned to Royma. "The dancing is starting. May I collect the dance you promised me?" he asked.

As her mother stood to leave for the dance floor, Moyra kicked Kellach hard under the table.

He looked up at her, startled. "Ouch, that hurt," he said.

"Ask me to dance," Moyra said through clenched teeth. She wanted to keep an eye on her mother and Fridjof.

"Moyra, you know that I don't like to—ouch!" Kellach rubbed his leg. "I mean, would you care to dance?"

"Why thank you, Kellach, I'd love to," she murmured. They joined the other dancers on the floor.

The music started and they began to twirl. Moyra led them around the dance floor, trying to stay close to her mother. She stumbled once and stepped on Kellach's feet. He winced in pain.

"Sorry, Kellach," she said, craning her neck to look for her mother. "I just want to keep an eye on my mom. I can't see them, can you?"

Just then, Fridjof whirled by with Royma, who was smiling. Her mother's face looked twenty years younger, carefree and happy. Over Royma's shoulder, Fridjof gave Moyra a triumphant grin.

Moyra looked away. "Let's go sit back down," she said.

"But the song's not over," Kellach protested.

"I know," Moyra said dully. "It doesn't matter. See how happy she is? Besides, I thought you hated to dance."

"It wasn't so bad," Kellach said. "Once I learned to avoid your clumsy feet."

Moyra didn't answer.

He poked Moyra's arm as they took their seats again. "What's wrong with you, Moyra? Aren't you going to yell at me for making a joke about you?"

"I don't feel well," Moyra said glumly. She didn't want to tell Kellach why. Fridjof had practically stolen her mother away. She was as good as an orphan now.

The song ended, and to her surprise, her mother returned to the table.

"You're back already?" Moyra couldn't keep the confusion from her voice. She thought her mother would have gladly danced with Fridjof all night.

"Yes, I am. It was a lovely dance," Royma said. She looked her daughter in the eye. "I love to dance, Moyra. That's all. And it's been so long since I have. You didn't seriously think I'd fall for Fridjof's false compliments, did you? I admit I enjoyed the attention, but I love your father. We'll always be a family."

Moyra jumped up and gave her mother a hug.

"Now," Royma turned to Kellach, "I saw you dancing out there with Moyra. Would you like to try it again with someone who really knows how to dance?"

Kellach looked a bit frightened, and Moyra and Driskoll laughed.

"Come on, Kell," Driskoll said. "You might learn something."

Kellach stood up reluctantly and scowled at his brother. "Okay, but you're next!"

Moyra watched her mother dance with Kellach and then Driskoll. Royma put her whole heart into it and the same look of joy was on her face, no matter who was her partner.

The music ended. There was a break in the dancing. Servants set out large bowls of punch and cups. Everyone returned to their seats or went to get something to drink.

A group of actors dressed all in black and wearing elaborate silver and gold masks appeared and took their places at the front of the room.

"A play," Royma said. She clapped her hands in delight. "I haven't been to a play in years."

Moyra turned her attention to the actors on stage. The play was a comedy, her favorite, but she couldn't seem to focus on what the actors were saying. She felt dizzy and looked down a moment to get her bearings.

When Moyra looked up again, Kellach was gone. The actors were no longer on stage, and Driskoll was talking. She shook her head. Had she fallen asleep?

"And there's cake with raspberries and cream." Driskoll groaned. "I wish I hadn't eaten that tenth gingerbread dragon." He pushed his plate away. "No more," he said firmly.

Moyra felt a slight buzz in her head, similar to the sound of an annoyed bumblebee. She grew dizzy again and put out a hand to steady herself. Maybe it was all that rich food.

"Moyra, are you okay?" Driskoll asked.

"I'm fine," she replied. But she didn't feel fine.

She took a deep breath. She took another breath. Her eyelids relaxed. Then she heard the voice in her head again.

Slip away. Don't let anyone notice.

Moyra's body seemed to have a will of its own. Without realizing what she was doing, she pushed her chair back and stood up.

She felt her heart pounding in her ears. What was happening to her? She commanded her feet to stop, but the voice in her head was louder now, repeating over and over. *Go upstairs.* She walked across the dance floor, moving as if in a dream.

She looked back over her shoulder. Royma was talking to Driskoll and hadn't even noticed Moyra had left.

Moyra opened her mouth to scream for help, but only a hoarse whisper came out.

Her feet took her toward the stairwell. People nodded and smiled as she went by, but no one stopped her to talk.

As she reached the staircase, her bilious green scarf fell from her neck.

She tried to lean down to pick it up. But her dress wouldn't move.

Suddenly, she realized it wasn't the food making her feel sick. It was the dress! The dress was enchanted. It felt as though it was pushing her, pushing her up the stairs.

Although she resisted with every bit of her willpower, her

feet continued to carry her away. Moyra knew she was headed for the gallery, but she didn't know why.

Moyra thought she caught a glimpse of Kellach standing near the huge ice sculptures of dragons frozen in battle. She shook her head violently. It was the only part of her body she could move freely. "Kellach!" she cried. But it came out as a whisper. He couldn't hear her. No one could.

Her feet carried her up the stairs and into the palace gallery.

Then suddenly the dress came to a halt.

Moyra stared at the shiny shelves filled with snow globes. It seemed there were even more now than there had been before.

Then Fridjof stepped out of the shadows.

CHAPTER

22

"Y ou!" Moyra said.

She was so astonished she didn't even realize her voice
had returned.

"Foolish girl, did you think you'd escape me?" Fridjof's
genial merchant mask was gone, replaced by a face twisted with
evil. "Give me the diamond."

"What diamond?" Moyra said, stalling for time. Her mind
raced.

"You are trying my patience." Fridjof's voice was like a blast
of cold air. "I've had enough of this foolishness. I've searched
everywhere for that diamond. I've tried bribing Zendric's apprentice. I tried searching your idiotic friend Driskoll—"

"But you . . . you saved Driskoll?" she stammered.

"Stupid child. I didn't save him." Fridjof sneered. "I caused
the hole in the ice to grow. I needed an excuse to search his pockets. I thought that perhaps he had the diamond. But, of course, that
was before I knew you had it . . . Now give me the diamond."

"How do you know I have it?" Moyra made her voice sound amazed and a little admiring. Maybe it would keep him talking in the hope that Kellach and Driskoll would eventually arrive to help her.

"You practically told me yourself when you asked if I bought unusual items. Besides, my servant Moli has been following you. Although he was not able to take it from you, I did ascertain that you kept it upon your person at all times. I simply had to bribe you with one of my enchanted dresses, and when the time was right, compel the dress to bring you to me. The feast was the perfect opportunity for you to wear it. I knew your greed wouldn't allow you to leave the dress behind." He smiled, and his voice turned high and sweet, mocking her. "Just once, you wanted to feel like a princess."

Moyra's felt her stomach sinking. How did he know?

Fridjof sneered. "You didn't think I noticed you at the market that day? The way you practically drooled over my wares?" He laughed. "You're like a pathetic puppy, you know that? You and your disgraceful mother. Always wanting what you can't have. You probably thought you could actually save your family by selling that diamond, didn't you? Buy a nice house in the Phoenix Quarter? Get your father out of prison?" Fridjof scoffed. "Fool. You'll never escape your roots."

Every bone in Moyra's body screamed to rush forward and punch Fridjof in the chest. She tried to lift her arms. But the dress held her fast. She felt like a fly hanging in a very sticky spider web.

"Now give it to me," he intoned.

Moyra gulped. Kellach was right. It was dangerous to carry the diamond around with her.

Finally, she found her voice again. "Why do you want it so badly? What's so special about one silly gem?"

Fridjof stepped closer and stared directly in her face. "It is the Diamond of Destruction."

"So?" Moyra asked innocently.

"You are rather slow, my dear," Fridjof said. "I want to use the diamond to destroy Curston."

"But why?" Moyra asked.

"Revenge, of course." Fridjof smiled. "What other reason is there? I've waited many years for this. Now, give it to me."

Moyra furiously shook her head. "Why do you hate Curston so much?" She flung the question at him.

"This town never appreciated my talents," Fridjof said, his face darkening. "Neither the town nor the Knights. I was the best wizard in the entire town, the entire region! But did the Knights acknowledge it? No."

"You're a wizard?" Moyra asked. Her voice dripped with fake astonishment. She'd do anything to keep him talking, even if it meant acting stupid. "But aren't you a merchant?"

Fridjof laughed, a frightening rumble deep in his throat. "Oh, my dear. You are a simple one, aren't you? Of course I'm a wizard. Where do you think I got all this food, all the toys, all the clothes? How do you think I built this ice palace? Why do you think Curston is suffering the coldest weather in over a hundred years?"

"That was you?"

"Of course it was me. I caused the cold snap. I sabotaged your wagon supplies. Then I rode heroically into town." Fridjof smiled fondly at the memory. "You were all so happy to see me. The savior of Curston." The wizard laughed. "How foolish of you."

"You . . . you can control the weather?" Moyra stalled. "But how?" She glanced back at the stairs. Come on, boys. Come on.

Fridjof narrowed his eyes. "Since leaving Curston, I have learned to control the very powers of nature! I have dominion over the ice and snow. The temperature will drop at my will. And there's nothing anyone can do to stop me!"

Fridjof stepped closer. "The Knights of the Silver Dragon always underestimated me. It was always Zendric they praised. In me, they saw only flaws. But I'm a better wizard than he ever was."

"Was?" Moyra said in alarm. "What do you mean?"

Fridjtof smiled, but he didn't answer her question. He held out his hand. "Give me the diamond."

Moyra gulped. "I don't have it any longer." Her voice trembled at the lie.

Fridjof's face turned dark with fury. He reached into the pocket of his ermine coat and carefully drew out a long wand. It was made of pure silver and at the top it had an empty setting, that looked just about the right size to hold the Diamond of Destruction.

"Give it to me or face the consequences." He pointed the wand down the long staircase. "Did you notice the new red dress your mother is wearing this evening? Well, it's a gift from me. Enchanted, of course. With one quick motion of my hand, I can force her to come up these stairs." Fridjof leaned in closer to Moyra. "But there's no telling if she will make it up here safely. Those stairs are made of ice. Quite slippery, you know. She might take a spill down the stairs. Perhaps she'll hit her head. Or break her leg? Do you really want to see your mother hurt?"

"No!" Moyra screamed. "You couldn't do that. You like my mother." With every word, she could feel her voice growing stronger. Was the enchantment on the dress wearing off?

"I merely used your mother . . . used her to get closer to what I need. Now, give me the diamond! If you don't have it, you know where it is."

"Yes, I'll give it to you," Moyra said. She couldn't stall any longer. She'd have to give Fridjof the diamond. "If you let me go and promise not to hurt my mother, I'll give it to you."

"Certainly." Fridjof's pale eyes gleamed.

"It's stitched into the hem of my dress."

Fridjof bent down and pulled roughly on the edge of Moyra's skirt. The stitches gave way easily, and the diamond tumbled into his hand.

Moyra tried not to betray her panic.

He held the diamond up to the light. "Beautiful, isn't it?" He placed it into the empty setting at the top of his wand. "Now I'm afraid you are no longer of any use to me," he said coldly.

"I . . . I thought you said you'd let me go."

Fridjof laughed. "There's no chance of that, girl. I can't have you alerting anyone to my plans."

Moyra cursed under her breath. She couldn't believe how gullible she'd been. She glanced back toward the stairs.

"I'm afraid it's no use to call out for help," Fridjof said. "By the time anyone finds you, it will be too late to save you or Curston. I've won."

"I don't think so," Kellach said as he strode into the room with his hand already tracing a spell in the air.

CHAPTER

23

S tand back, Moyra," Kellach said.

"We're here to save you!" Driskoll stepped out from behind his brother.

Moyra tried to move, then she realized she was still held fast by magic. "I'm spellbound. I can't move unless he wants me to."

Fridjof said, "Are you willing to bet your friend's life on this battle, young wizard?"

Kellach put down his hand. He was pale and panting.

Fridjof strolled up to him with a triumphant sneer. "If you would have continued, your friend would have been the one knocked unconscious. I could have channeled your spell directly to her."

Moyra looked at Kellach. "How did you know where to find me?"

"The scarf was a great clue," Kellach said. "Driskoll thought it was a signal for help."

Driskoll smiled. "I figured it out even before Kellach did."

Kellach turned to Fridjof. "Why did you pretend to be a merchant?" he asked. "You're a wizard."

Fridjof gave a bow. "A wizard and a Knight of the Silver Dragon."

Driskoll drew in a sharp gasp. "You? You're a Knight?"

Fridjof nodded. "I was until Zendric banished me to the Far North."

"That explains the Knight of the Silver Dragon pin Torin found in the missing supply wagon." Moyra's eyes narrowed. "Fridjof sabotaged the wagons and left the pin there to frame Zendric."

Fridjof laughed sickly. "Well, child, you are clever after all. Yes, I sabotaged the wagons and I hoped that they would blame my old rival. How was I to know that Zendric would have gone running as soon as he sensed my presence in Curston. The coward." Fridjof fairly spat the word. "But, no matter. I have taken care of him."

"What have you done to him?" Moyra tried to wriggle free of the dress's spellhold, but it was as if a giant's hand was wrapped around her, squeezing tight. She still couldn't move. "We're not going to let you get away with this, Fridjof."

"Children," Fridjof snarled. "What can you children do to stop me? I will destroy the town. I'm simply waiting for the rest of the Knights of the Silver Dragon to reveal themselves."

Moyra exchanged glances with Kellach. Fridjof had been in town all this time and he didn't know that Zendric had made them Knights of the Silver Dragon?

"We are the Knights of the Silver Dragon," Kellach said, moving closer to his brother, "We are the only Knights left besides Zendric."

Fridjof laughed, his voice sounding like the howl of a winter wind. He stopped laughing abruptly. "How the mighty have fallen."

"Zendric is twice the wizard you'll ever be," Moyra cried.

"I don't think so," Fridjof said, his lips twisting viciously. "Zendric is dead, girl."

Moyra looked at Kellach in horror.

Kellach whispered to her, "There's still hope."

Just then, they heard footsteps coming up the stairs. Kalmbur burst through the door of the gallery. "Driskoll, Kellach, your father has been looking everywhere for you—"

He froze mid-sentence as Fridjof waved his hand. In his place, there was a small snow globe.

Moyra stared at the globe, unable to help herself. Inside it was a miniature version of Kalmbur. He still had his mouth open as if he wanted to finish his sentence.

Moyra took in a sharp breath. "I told you that half-orc wagon driver looked familiar. He *looked* like the figure in the snow globe because he *was* that figure in the snow globe."

Driskoll stared at the shelves and shelves with snow globes. "You mean these were all once real people? And real animals?"

Moyra nodded. "They're all victims of Fridjof."

"I prefer to call them my conquests." Fridjof said smugly. He lifted one of the globes off its shelf and stroked the smooth glass. "Beautiful, isn't it? It's such a pleasure to keep a record of all the fools I've conquered."

"You're not going to get away with this," Driskoll said. "My dad will come looking for us soon."

"Let him come. If he does, he will become part of my collection." Fridjof replaced the globe onto the icy shelf. "Now where are the Knights? I grow impatient with these interruptions. I am ready to enact my revenge."

Driskoll stomped his foot. "We told you! We are the Knights."

Fridjof shook his head. "Very well, children, if you insist on dying without telling me where they are . . . " He chanted under his breath, closing his eyes and concentrating deeply.

Moyra tried to move her foot, and to her surprise, she had control of her limbs again. She looked at Fridjof, but he was still deep in a spell trance. She edged closer to Kellach, careful to walk slowly and quietly.

"What is he doing?" she asked in a whisper.

"From the look of it, casting a powerful spell. That's why you are able to move again. He needs every bit of his strength for whatever spell it is," Kellach replied.

"Let's get out of here!" Driskoll said. "While he's busy."

Kellach said, "No, I need to stop him. Whatever he's doing, it can't be good."

"You're too late." Fridjof snapped out of his trance.

"You won't get away with this," Moyra cried.

"The creature will be here shortly," he continued. "And all of Curston will rue the day the Knights threw me out."

"Not if I have anything to say about it," Kellach said. A bolt of green magic leaped from his hand.

CHAPTER

24

Fridjof muttered under his breath, and suddenly a shield of silver magic flew out in front of him.

The two streams of energy battled, but it was clear that Kellach would not be able to withstand the powerful wizard for long.

"There's no point in fighting me, boy!" Fridjof crowed. He lifted his wand with the Diamond of Destruction in its tip. "Your girlfriend gave me the diamond. And I'm prepared to use it." The diamond began to glow with blue light.

Out of the corner of her eye, Moyra saw a movement in the shadows. "Kellach, be careful!" she said.

But it was too late.

Moli, Fridjof's dwarf servant, leaped on Kellach and knocked him to the floor. They hit the icy floor and slid uncontrollably, crashing directly into Fridjof's legs.

Fridjof fell flat on his face, and the wand flew out of his hand. It ricocheted off the wall, sending rays of blue magic bouncing around the room.

"Moli, you idiot!" Fridjof cried. "Look what you've done." He tried to stand, but he couldn't seem to find his feet on the slippery floor.

The wand's blue magic shattered everything it touched.

"Look out!" Kellach cried as he struggled against the dwarf's strong grip.

The elaborately carved ice paintings shook free and came crashing down. The walls of the palace began to crumble. Sharp shards of ice whizzed by their heads. An icicle rocketed off one wall and skewered Moli's right sleeve, pinning him to the ground.

Kellach broke free from the dwarf and scrambled to his feet.

"We've got to get out of here!" Moyra cried.

The walls of the ice palace shook.

"But what about Fridjof's victims?" Driskoll asked, gesturing to the rows of snow globes. "They'll be killed if they're not returned to their living forms."

"Let them," Fridjof said with a sneer. He gripped an icicle and plunged it into the cracking wall, using the leverage to pull himself up.

Moyra's eyes flew wide. "I know where Zendric is!" She frantically began picking up globes, one by one, and peering closely inside them.

Kellach immediately understood. "He's in one of the snow globes!"

"Quick! Help me look! We don't have much time." As she spoke, the icy floor began to crack beneath her feet.

She had gone through all the globes on the far wall and was

about to start on a new shelf when she let out a gasp. "I found it!" She shoved the glass globe in Kellach's hand. "This is it! It's Zendric. Can you get him out?"

"I can try," he said. He concentrated, muttering under his breath.

But nothing happened.

"It's not working! You've got to get out of here now! I'll follow you."

"No! Kellach, you'll be killed," Moyra cried.

"Just go and take as many globes as you can carry!" Kellach replied.

"Do what you like," Fridjof sneered, standing in front of them. "It won't help you or the town."

Fridjof handed the wand to Moli to carry, and they started for the stairs. Moyra thought that, powerful sorcerer or not, Fridjof was afraid of the havoc he and his minions had created. He was running a little too quickly for an invincible wizard.

The palace walls buckled and shook. Great chunks of ice rained down on their heads. The shaking grew worse. They heard the cries of the panic-stricken townspeople rushing to get out. Moyra and Driskoll rushed to the stairs to look at the scene below. It was absolute chaos.

"Moyra, where are you?" Royma's voice came above the crowd.

"Mom, I'm up here!" Moyra called. "Get out now! I'll find you outside."

Moyra saw Torin, barking orders, trying to guide the towns-people out of the palace. "Single file. Everyone stay calm."

But no one was.

People were punching and clawing to get outside. Moyra saw a little pixie almost crushed by a half-orc as he barreled through the crowd to reach the door. A couple of elves jumped out a first floor window, and others soon followed suit.

Kellach said, "Moyra, you need to make a run for it. The palace is ready to shatter. I'm almost there. I can feel it."

Moyra nodded. She and Driskoll filled their arms with snow globes, and then they dashed down the staircase as it buckled and twisted. Moyra's dress caught on the banister rail. She was caught fast.

Without thinking twice, she ripped her gown free. The force sent the banister crashing down. She quickly jumped the few remaining steps. The stairs disintegrated mere seconds later.

As she raced across the dance floor, she was glad to see the main room was empty. She looked down at her dress, wincing only a little to see the tear she had created in the beautiful fabric. It hurt her to tear into the first lovely dress she ever owned, but it was ruined now anyway.

Icicles rained down on her as she ran, forcing her to take a zigzag path toward the exit.

"Be careful of the ice!" she called over her shoulder at Driskoll.

At last, they made it to the front doors. But the door was blocked by Grellen. He was juggling two roast turkeys and a cake, trying to make it out the door without slipping.

"Drop it!" Moyra shouted. "This whole place is about to come down."

The building shook and more pieces of ice fell down on them, but the stubborn half-orc refused to listen.

Then came the sound of shattering ice.

Driskoll looked up and pointed. "The ceiling! It's coming down!"

With that, Grellen broke off a drumstick, dropped the turkeys and the cake on the floor, and ran for his life.

CHAPTER

25

Moyra stood at the front of the crowd of townspeople, watching as the ice palace came crashing down.

When nothing was left but a pile of icy rubble, she dared to look behind her.

She was relieved to see her mother huddled near Torin. The captain of the watch looked shell-shocked, but he was still barking orders.

"There's nothing left to see here!" he called. "Everyone return to Curston immediately!"

Drivers pulled up their wagons, and the townspeople pushed and shoved, desperate to get a seat and be home as quickly as possible.

"One at a time!" Torin bellowed. "There is room for everyone!"

Some people didn't wait for a wagon and began to trudge out of the clearing and onto the main thoroughfare.

"It looks like all of Curston made it out of the palace safely," Driskoll said softly as they set the rescued snow globes on the icy ground.

"All but Kellach and Zendric," Moyra intoned. She hung her head and gritted her teeth, trying to keep the tears from falling.

"Where's Fridjof?" Driskoll stood on his tiptoes, trying to catch a glimpse above the frantic crowd. "And his dwarves? I don't see them anywhere."

Moyra heard a sound like the distant rumble of thunder. Then came a keening sound so loud and sharply pitched that it hurt her ears to hear it.

"What's that?" Driskoll shouted.

Whatever it was, it shook the snowy clearing so hard, that the snowflakes seemed to defy gravity and fly back up in the air.

"That doesn't sound like any storm I've ever heard," Moyra said. She put her hands over her ears as the ground shook even harder. She struggled to stay on her feet. "It must be an earthquake. We've got to get out of here."

But there was no time left to run.

With an ear-splitting crack, the ground by the ice palace erupted, spewing forth a flurry of ice and snow.

And when the snow settled, there stood the most disgusting creature Moyra had ever seen.

The creature looked like an enormous millipede, its pale blue skin pulsing with a red glow. As the beast pulled itself out of the icy hole, its dozens of insectoid legs chattered, and its back bristled with a pair of winglike fins.

"Remorhaz!" someone shouted. The crowd screamed and began to push out of the clearing.

"What's a remorhaz?" Moyra asked. "I've never heard of it before."

"That's because one has never been seen in these parts," Driskoll replied. "They normally live in arctic climates. Fridjof must have called it just before the palace collapsed."

As the remorhaz took in its surroundings, its two pairs of antennae whirled. It trained its faceted eyes, as large as silver platters, on the crowd.

"By Harrid's horns!" Driskoll cried. "Look at that thing!"

"It's like an oven out here," Moyra said. It was weird. First it was freezing, now it was hot?

"A remorhaz generates the heat of a hundred bonfires," Fridjof said, stepping in front of them.

Moli, the dwarf, followed behind him, with a sneer plastered on his face. "There is no hope for you now."

"Quick, Driskoll, think!" Moyra tugged on her friend's jacket. "What can we do to fight a remorhaz?"

Driskoll wrung his hands. "I don't know. I've only read about them. Kellach would know. Where is he?"

Moyra glanced back at the icy rubble and her heart ached. Poor Kellach. Poor Zendric.

Fridjof's lips twisted into a vicious smile. "There's nothing to do now but watch. Watch as the remorhaz lays waste to your people." Fridjof laughed. "The Knights of the Silver Dragon will remember my name."

The remorhaz's entire body contracted as its dozens of legs

pushed it forward. Its antennae reached out and brushed against Grellen, who was so busy nibbling on the drumstick he had forgotten to run.

The remorhaz reared up to strike. The half-orc leaped backward and fell into a snow drift. The creature's wide mouth opened to reveal row after row of jagged teeth.

"Stop it!" Driskoll yelled.

"Why should I?" Fridjof said.

"Moyra!" Driskoll shouted. "We have to do something!"

Moyra knew there was no way they could kill the remorhaz in time to save Grellen. But, she thought, there was one thing she could do.

"Grellen!" Moyra hollered. She lifted her skirt and pulled the knife out of the holster on her leg. "Catch!"

The knife flew through the air and landed on the snowbank next to the half-orc. Grellen gripped it. And then the remorhaz leaned forward and swallowed him whole.

"Clever child," Fridjof said. "You may have just saved that half-orc's life, if he's not too stupid to figure out what the knife is for."

While Fridjof stared intently at the remorhaz, Moyra kept her eyes on the silver wand, with its diamond tip, poking out of a pocket of Moli's silver cloak.

Moyra stepped closer as casually as possible. Did she dare to try it? She squared her shoulders. It was time to truly test her skills as a thief.

Driskoll edged closer to her, trying not to attract Fridjof's attention. "What are you doing?" he whispered.

"I just need another minute. Keep Fridjof busy, okay?"

She gripped a piece of ice from the ruined palace in her hand, then she meandered over to Moli, who was still engrossed in the remorhaz.

Moyra's hands danced fast as lightning over the wand. There was a flash of blue as her hands stilled. Moyra froze, but no one was paying any attention to her. She took two steps back.

Fridjof called out, "Moli, mind the wand! It's about to fall out of your pocket! Do I have to do everything around here?"

"Sorry, master," the dwarf said, pulling the wand out of his pocket and wrapping his short arms around it. "But what are we waiting for?"

"Something you don't get to see too often." Fridjof chuckled. "I don't believe it. The half-orc evidently does possess a modicum of intelligence."

Moyra turned to look. Good Grellen, she thought.

The tip of Moyra's blade stuck halfway out of the center of the remorhaz's body. The beast reared up and screeched. Moyra's hands flew up to cover her ears as she watched her knife slice a hole down the length of the creature's body.

The hole split open, and Grellen fell out of the creature's steaming body. He was covered in clumpy goo, but, otherwise, he appeared unharmed.

The creature reared up again. But this time it was not in fury, but in pain. Its antennae whirled, and its legs beat aimlessly at the air.

Moyra smiled. The beast was about to die.

But then something astonishing happened.

The wound in the remorhaz's belly closed before her eyes, like an eyelid winking shut. The remorhaz crashed to the ground and let out a frightening screech.

"Unbelievable!" Moyra said. "It's still alive!"

Grellen took one last look at the beast and ran into the woods, screaming. The remorhaz slithered after him, but Fridjof waved his hand and the creature froze.

"Well, that was amusing. But now, we have work to do." He snapped his fingers. "Moli, my wand."

The dwarf handed the wand to Fridjof. The diamond at the tip seemed to sparkle in the light.

Moyra held her breath. Would it be enough to fool Fridjof? Moyra hoped so. If not, Curston was doomed.

Driskoll said, "It's not too late to change your mind. You were a Knight once. You don't have to do this."

"Do you think I'm an imbecile?" Fridjof whirled on Driskoll, his face contorted in anger. "I know I don't have to do it. I want to. At last I'll get my revenge on Zendric and the Knights of the Silver Dragon. They'll regret kicking me out of their precious order."

Fridjof held his hand over the diamond and began chanting under his breath.

Driskoll gasped. "We have to stop him," he said. He launched himself at the wizard, but Moyra grabbed his jacket.

"Wait," Moyra whispered.

Driskoll arched an inquiring eyebrow at Moyra. She gave him a tiny nod.

He pointed the wand in the direction of Curston. "Any

moment now, the Knights shall feel my wrath." Fridjof seemed to brace himself. "Any moment now," he repeated.

But nothing happened.

Fridjof pulled back the wand and examined the diamond closely. He put his hand over the diamond and recoiled at the cool sting of plain ice.

"You little thief!" He snarled at Moyra. "It's a piece of ice! You stole my diamond while I wasn't looking and replaced it with a piece of ice!"

Moyra shrugged, holding up the diamond. "It fooled you, didn't it?"

"Only for a moment." Fridjof scoffed and ripped the diamond out of Moyra's hands.

Moyra gasped.

"You *children* don't seem to understand that you cannot fight against me. I am a wizard!" Fridjof's chest puffed out as he spoke. "You two are no match for me. I conquered Zendric easily. And your little wizard boyfriend?" Fridjof scoffed. "A failure."

Moyra's face flamed at the mention of Kellach. "He managed to battle with you, didn't he? He fought well."

Driskoll said, "He's a better wizard than you'll ever be. And we're Knights of the Silver Dragon. We'll find a way to stop you, I know we will."

"Try stopping this." Fridjof released the remorhaz from its frozen state.

The ground rumbled as the creature began to move again. Its legs chittered against the frozen snow. It turned its head and trained its platter-shaped eyes directly on Moyra and Driskoll.

Fridjof laughed. "I've had quite enough of your meddling."

Moyra and Driskoll gulped.

The remorhaz reared up and opened its mouth, preparing to swallow them whole.

CHAPTER

26

Moyra closed her eyes and tensed her body, preparing for the inevitable.

"The creature is under my command," Fridjof sneered. "In a matter of seconds, you and Driskoll will be destroyed."

"I don't think so," a voice said.

Moyra couldn't believe her ears. "Zendric?"

She opened her eyes. The remorhaz was frozen again, its mouth still partly opened. It lilted from one side to the other, and then it fell to the ground with an ear-deafening crash.

"What h-happened?" Driskoll stammered when the ground stopped shaking. "Is-is it dead?"

"No, a simple sleep spell." Zendric strode out from behind a large chunk of ice, with Kellach right behind him. "But that should do the trick for the time being."

"Kellach!" Driskoll threw his arms around his brother. "You're alive!" Driskoll's head whipped over to Zendric, and he smiled. "You're both alive!"

Moyra hung her head. "I'm sorry, Zendric. We tried to stop him."

"You've done very well, Moyra," Zendric said and put a hand on her shoulder. Zendric's wizard robes flowed behind him.

"Zendric," Fridjof hissed the name. He seemed smaller somehow, standing before Zendric. "How did you get out of the globe? Your apprentice couldn't possibly have—"

"Oh, but he did," Zendric said. "We made it out of the palace before it crumbled, but we made sure that you didn't see us. Before revealing myself, I felt it prudent to see what my old friend was up to."

"Old friend?" Fridjof's pale face reddened in anger. "You dare to call me a friend?"

"We were friends, Fridjof," Zendric said sadly. "Until you betrayed me and your duty as a Knight of the Silver Dragon."

"Duty?" Fridjof sneered. "What duty? The Knights never wanted *me*."

"You were a valuable member of our order, Fridjof," Zendric said. "That is, until you tried to steal the Diamond of Destruction."

Moyra stepped forward, pointing at Fridjof. "It was you? You stole the diamond?" She looked back at Zendric. "Zendric, why in the god's darkest names, did you take the blame?"

Zendric sighed. "I admit it was foolish. But it was a long time ago. We all make mistakes."

"What happened?" Driskoll asked.

"It wasn't long after the Knights had confiscated the Diamond of Destruction," Zendric explained. "We kept the jewel in a secret stronghold, and as far as the people of Curston knew, I was the only who held the key. No one knew I had entrusted Fridjof with the secret as well. He was a young wizard then. My first apprentice."

Fridjof grimaced at the memory.

Zendric continued, "I had no idea my young apprentice hungered for the power the Diamond could offer. Thankfully, I noticed it was gone and was able to recover it before any real damage was done.

"But I was ashamed . . . ashamed that my own apprentice could be capable of such treachery. I didn't want anyone to know how I had failed him. I feared people would never trust their children to apprentice with me again. So, I hid the truth. Curston was already aware that the Diamond had been stolen. The Knights simply let the townspeople continue to believe it, so no one would go looking for it again. Then we tucked it away in the eaves of the cathedral."

Moyra nodded. "Until it came crashing down on me."

Zendric nodded. "And with the blessing of the other Knights, I banished Fridjof to the Far North."

"But you never dreamed I'd return." Fridjof's head whipped around, scanning the clearing. "Now where are the rest of the Knights?"

"As my friends have undoubtedly told you," Zendric said, "you have met the new generation of the Knights of the Silver Dragon. Aside from me, they're the only ones left."

"I don't believe it!" Fridjof said. "You mean these children were telling the truth? All that remains of the great and glorious

Knights are three children and an old man? Hah! Then I suppose you alone will have to pay for their sins."

Fridjof waved his hand, and a baseball-sized piece of hail rained down on Zendric's head. The old wizard ducked, but the hail caught him on the side of his head. A trickle of blood ran down his face.

"What's wrong with him?" Moyra whispered to Kellach. "Why isn't he fighting back?"

"Zendric is still very weak from being imprisoned in the globe," Kellach said in a low voice. "He couldn't even cast the sleep spell on the remorhaz. I had to do it for him."

Fridjof sneered, "I see you are too much of a coward to fight me, Zendric."

"Give up, Fridjof," Zendric said calmly. "You cannot stand against the Knights of the Silver Dragon." He glanced at Kellach out of the corner of his eye.

Fridjof threw his head back and laughed. "You must be kidding." He tapped his wand on the ground, clearing out the chunk of ice stuck in the wand's setting. Then he replaced it with the Diamond of Destruction. "I have been dreaming of this moment for years. My revenge is nearly complete. A weak old man and three children will not stop me."

Driskoll's eyes went wide "What are we going to do? If Zendric is powerless, then there's no hope!"

"Not exactly." Kellach smiled. He pulled the fire amulet out from beneath his tunic.

Moyra and Driskoll instantly understood his meaning. Moyra gripped the hoop still hanging from her ear. Driskoll pulled a dark stone out of his jacket pocket.

Fridjof held the wand aloft, the diamond sparkling in the moonlight. "This wand has more power than you ever possessed, my friend. Say good-bye to Curston, Zendric."

Together, Moyra, Kellach, and Driskoll aimed their amulets at the frost wizard.

"Emalf!" they all shouted at once.

Three bolts of fire shot out from the amulets, striking Fridjof directly in the chest. The wand flew of his hands as the force of the amulets knocked the wizard backward and into one of the ruined walls of the ice palace.

Zendric picked up the wand and tucked it into his pocket. He turned to face his young friends.

"Thank you for your assistance, Knights. You have done well." Zendric smiled, taking in the sight of Fridjof's defeated form. The wizard had slumped over a chunk of ice, unconscious. A thin trail of smoke sizzled up out of his hair. "Very well indeed."

CHAPTER

27

The next day, as Driskoll, Kellach, and Moyra strolled through Curston's Main Square, Moyra couldn't help but smile.

The ice and snow had already melted into huge puddles. The artic wind that had chilled Curston's citizens to the bone was gone. She could hear the birds chirping and feel the warm sun beat on her back.

Moyra ran ahead, relishing the feeling of wearing pants again. Her mother had sewn up the tear in her pants. It had been nice to feel pretty for one day, but given all the trouble the dress had caused, she was glad to be back in her normal clothes.

The market was crowded, as usual. But this time, the merchants had plenty to sell. Moyra sidled up to the sweets stand, with Driskoll and Kellach right behind her.

"You know what I missed during all this?" she asked.

"Chocolate cake?" Driskoll guessed.

"Brownies," Kellach said with conviction.

"No, I missed hot chocolate. The hotter the better," said Moyra as she handed them cups of steaming, rich, hot chocolate.

"Is there one of those for me?" Zendric's deep voice boomed from behind her.

Moyra whirled around. "Zendric!"

Kellach rushed over to the wizard. "Are you feeling better?"

Zendric stretched his arms. "Much better, my friends. A good night's rest and all is well with the world again."

Driskoll reached into his pocket and drew out his fire amulet. "I guess you'd like these back now."

Moyra and Kellach offered theirs as well, but Zendric shook his head. "Keep them. You never know when you may need them. But promise me you will only use them when you truly need them."

"I have a question, Zendric," Moyra said as she paid the elf maiden behind the counter for one more cup of hot chocolate. "How did you know we would find the amulets?"

"I didn't." Zendric grabbed the cup and took a sip. "I only hoped you would. It was all outlined clearly in the book I gave to Kellach."

Moyra smirked and prodded Kellach good-naturedly. "I think you may need to give your apprentice here a few remedial lessons in Elvish."

Kellach scowled. "I got us through it, didn't I?"

Driskoll set his cup on the counter and wiped the chocolate mustache off his upper lip. "But how did you know Fridjof would be coming to Curston, Zendric?"

"I was suspicious when the weather turned unseasonably cold," Zendric said. "But when Royma told me there were rumors of winter wolves circling Curston's walls, then I knew Fridjof must be on his way. The wolves were his familiars, you see."

Driskoll slapped his forehead. "Of course! There were wolves all over the ice palace. We should have known."

"I had had word from the North that Fridjof had been gathering his powers," Zendric continued. "There, he had become a full-fledged frost wizard. And I knew the only way to defeat him was the fire amulets. But it was too dangerous for me to recover them."

"Why?" Moyra asked.

"Fridjof wanted to destroy Curston. But most of all, he wanted to destroy me."

Driskoll looked up at the old wizard. "Were you scared?"

"No." Zendric put a hand on Driskoll's shoulder. "But it had been many years since I last saw Fridjof and he had changed since then. I had to draw him out to test the extent of his powers."

"Sometimes it's better to wait for your opponent to make a mistake," Moyra said, "like when I play cards."

Zendric nodded. "I rushed home to my tower. When I looked in my seeing stone, I saw a figure in the frost. Then I knew I had to make my way to the safe house."

"You mean the room in the Flying Dragon?" Kellach asked.

"Thelonius!" Moyra exclaimed. "We thought he was the one who had you imprisoned."

"No, Thelonius helped me to remain hidden. He is a guardian."

The three kids looked up at the wizard quizzically.

Zendric tilted his head to one side and stared down at the three Knights. "I thought I had explained this to all of you?"

Kellach shook his head. "No, I'm sure of it."

Zendric sighed. "A guardian is someone who protects the secrets of our order. Whenever a Knight or a guardian passes an important piece of information between them, they speak the words, 'Guard it well.'"

Moyra took in a quick breath. "That's what you said when you gave Kellach the amulet book! And when Thelonius gave us a book about the Knights' history."

"He was kind of grumpy for a friend of the Knights," Driskoll said, wrinkling his nose.

Zendric laughed. "Yes, but you can always turn to Thelonius in times of need. I thought you would understand from my final message that you were to deliver the amulets to him. But when he told me you claimed you hadn't found them, I decided I would have to recover them myself after all."

"And then Fridjof captured you," Kellach prompted.

Zendric nodded. "I had planned to use the tunnels to travel to the ruins and recover the first amulet, the most powerful of the three. But I should have known Fridjof would remember our tunnels. He used the frost worm to block me. And then he enchanted me into the snow globe." Zendric smiled wryly. "I taught him well."

"Gods!" Moyra cried. "The frost worm! Do you think it's still down there?"

Zendric pointed up at the warm blue sky and shook his head.

"Not to worry, my dear. Creatures of the frost cannot survive in this climate. The frost worm and the remorhaz are long gone by now. We won't see them again."

Driskoll crossed his arms in front of his chest. "What about Fridjof?"

Kellach answered for Zendric. "Dad has him locked up in the darkest corner of Curston's prison. He won't see the light of day . . . or a snowflake . . . for many years to come."

"And Kalmbur?" Moyra remembered seeing the kind watcher frozen in the snow globe. She shivered.

"Good as new." Zendric smiled. "I managed to restore all of Fridjof's victims."

Moyra breathed deeply, taking in the smells of fresh bread and sweet ripe fruit and watching the crowd mill past them. A young elf crunched into a bright green apple as he walked down the row of merchants' tents. A dwarf merchant burst into laughter after his customer finished a silly joke.

She turned back to her friends. "I can't believe we came so close to losing all this."

"I know." Zendric inhaled deeply. "I never imagined that Fridjof would try to retrieve the Diamond of Destruction."

"I'm sorry." Moyra hung her head. "It was my fault. I almost destroyed Curston. I wish I'd never found the diamond."

Zendric put his hand on her head. "No, my friend. You are wrong. It was you who saved Curston. If you hadn't hesitated to sell the diamond, Fridjof might have won. He underestimated your character."

Driskoll put his arm around her shoulder. "You were a hero!"

"A true Knight." Kellach smiled.

Moyra looked down, her face reddening. She stuffed her hand in her pocket and felt a sharp pin prick her finger. "Oh! I almost forgot." She drew out the dragon pin. "We found this in the tunnels."

"Thank the gods!" Zendric said, leaning over and allowing Moyra to attach the pin to the front of his robes. "I thought it was lost forever."

Moyra patted Zendric's shoulder, and he stood up again to his full height.

"Much better," Zendric said, clapping his hands. "Now, we need to discuss what you would like to do with the diamond."

Moyra looked up in surprise. "The diamond belongs to the Knights of the Silver Dragon. It wouldn't be right for me to keep it," she said.

Zendric put one hand on his hip. "It is very valuable but also very powerful. The diamond is the property of the Knights of the Silver Dragon, and you have seen what that kind of power can do if placed in the wrong hands. I will lock it away in my tower."

Zendric thought for a moment. "There was, if I remember correctly, a reward for its return. It will not bring you the riches you would have gained if you had sold it, but the reward should be enough so that you and your mother don't have to work quite so hard."

Zendric drew out a money pouch and placed it in Moyra's hands. "Guard it well." He winked at Moyra and disappeared into the crowd.

Driskoll drained his cup of chocolate and set it down. "I can't believe it's all over. What will we do for excitement now?"

"Don't worry, Driskoll," Kellach said. "Zendric did give us the fire amulets. He must be expecting us to use them again. I don't think this is the last adventure we'll have."

"No, it's not over." Moyra gripped the money pouch, a broad smile on her face. "I think it's just beginning for the Knights of the Silver Dragon."

KNIGHTS of the SILVER DRAGON™

A YOUNG THIEF.

A WIZARD'S APPRENTICE.

A 12 YEAR-OLD BOY.

MEET THE KNIGHTS OF
THE SILVER DRAGON!

SECRET OF THE SPIRITKEEPER
Matt Forbeck

Can Moyra, Kellach, and Driskoll unlock the secret of the
spiritkeeper in time to rescue their beloved wizard friend?

RIDDLE IN STONE
Ree Soesbee

Will the knights unravel the statue's riddle
before more people turn to stone?

SIGN OF THE SHAPESHIFTER
Dale Donovan

Can Kellach and Driskoll find the shapeshifter
before he ruins their father?

EYE OF FORTUNE
Denise Graham

Does the fortuneteller's prophecy spell doom
for the knights? Or unheard-of treasure?

For ages 8 to 12